RHODES
NEVER FORGOTTEN

RHODES

NEVER FORGOTTEN

M. M. Gornell

Champlain Avenue Books, Inc.
Novella Imprint
Las Vegas, Nevada

International Standard Book Number ISBN- 978-1-943063-60-4

FIRST EDITION
2021

Printed in the United States of America

In Memory of:

Marie Jones Griffin, Frank Jones, and Fred Jones

PREFACE

For some, the unknown future is far more interesting than past or present realities. The Mojave Desert, especially along Route 66, offers endless possibilities for exploration into past happenings, for experiencing the intensity of the desert environment in the present, and for positing unknown futures. And of course, for creating fanciful fiction spanning all time periods.

PROLOGUE

Did Sister Luke see me slip out of morning Mass?

Dominic knew she was always watching them—*him* in particular. And he prayed to God that Sister Luke saw him leave, and would be coming to his rescue soon. He was afraid though, based on his catechism class lessons, that saving him from Tony might not be a *holy* enough reason for Godly intervention.

Nonetheless, he continued praying and hoping. *Please, Sister, come soon.*

In the meantime, he had to escape Mass to avoid their evilness; so for now, the small bathroom by the gym would have to do as his hideout. Urgent student bathroom callings during Mass were allowed—but if you stayed too long...

Please, Sister, come soon...come soon.

Unfortunately, the bathroom was even colder than the always-freezing high-ceiling gym where Mass was being held. Dominic figured the bathroom coldness was because of all the tiny white bathroom tiles soaking up the heat produced by the one aged and noisy radiator near the sink. Adding to the heat-sucking tiles, he also thought the bathroom's two single-pained windows—placed way up high near the ceiling so you couldn't see in from outside— barely let any sunrays in, and were actually acting as one-way heating-vents from the bathroom to the twenty-degree Chicago winter morning outside.

Indeed, hiding in the last stall, and shivering slightly, he had unconsciously wrapped his thin arms around his chest—and unheard by his own ears, Dominic was now starting to moan very slightly from the chill. And fear. And loneliness.

He did for sure know, Sister Luke had not seen Tony jab him in the butt from behind with that protractor of his. Dominic had almost cried out in pain. His nemesis was good at terrorizing him like that, and without Sister catching on.

I hate him and his little club. He figured they were all smirking right now.

When it came to evil-doers in general, Dominic's mother and father talked about Karma, and Father James talked about hell waiting for sinners. He, however, dreamed of payback in *this* world.

"I'll never forget," Dominic whispered, hugging himself even tighter, while warm salty tears began to fill and burn his nearsighted seven-year-old eyes. "One day."

His hidey-hole nook was to the side of the toilet in the last stall in a row of six—and even more icy cold than the rest of the boy's lavatory. Nonetheless, it was his favorite escape spot in the aged brick building because of the special tiled ledge to the side of the toilet where he could prop up and hide his feet.

Mass in the gym will be over in a few more minutes, Dominic thought. Then classes would start about ten minutes after that. With the start of English class, Sister Aquinas would come looking for him for sure—*even if Sister Luke doesn't come, Aquinas will come and save me.*

Yep, Dominic knew he was Sister Aquinas's favorite pupil—always calling on him to report on their latest

English lesson. Her favoritism towards him in class often caused his cheeks to burn. For as Sister also loved pointing out to the class, Dominic was named after a Saint who founded some Priest's order he didn't really know much about—except for the name. *Dominicans.*

Suddenly, Dominic felt like crying grownup style— with big tears and sobs, not just silly kid-tears—but he knew he shouldn't do that right now. *Too much of a baby and weakling thing to do.* And someone might hear him. He certainly didn't want either Sister Luke or Sister Aquinas to find him crying.

Instead, to distract himself while he waited to be rescued, Dominic pulled his tightly-rolled-up section of the Chicago Tribune out of its special inside compartment in the satchel he always had with him. No one knew he read a newspaper every day—and Dominic wanted to keep it that way. They already called him "four-eyes," "purse carrier," and "snooty"—*if they knew I read the newspaper on top of that....*

He also had hidden even farther away inside his rolled-up Tribune section, his mother's Sun Times page containing Ann Lander's column—secreted away for forced escape times like this. When reading her daily column—for a short time he would often find solace in knowing about grownup problems. He'd imagine he was an adult, and away from all this. He'd be married and have children— though he couldn't *really* imagine what that was like—even with Ann Lander's insights.

But for sure, not like my little problems. He was just a kid. But one day, he would be a grownup, too, and wouldn't be hiding in the bathroom like a scared little boy. Dominic sniffed hard enough for it to hurt inside his nostrils, causing him to swipe and blow his nose with the handkerchief his mother always tucked away for him inside his uniform-jacket pocket. With that, his nose hurt even worse, causing him to tear-up even more.

Quite philosophically for a child his age, Dominic figured times like this would *never* be *completely* forgotten— but he hoped and prayed by the time he grew up and had "Ann Lander's column type problems," this morning would be just a bad memory.

Chapter One

Before Leigh "Leiv" Everett Rhodes Knew Anything Was Going On

From LC's journal: *I still remember them early days — heading out west, looking for a life of my own away from them darned Coopers in Chicago. Not that I'd want to go back now. But them days when I was a young pup were something alright. Starting a new life out here in the west is the best thing I ever done. Do say, though, had to do me a lot of singing way back then to keep me moving along the road. Felt like giving up a lot a times. But then I'd sing me that churchy marching hymn and just keep on going....*

Early Friday Morning: *In a small Mercedes Touring Coach, side emblazoned D&D Tours, and having started out from Santa Monica Pier, California, their van was now en route—heading east on I-40, a little east of Ludlow*

"Glory, glory, halleluiah," Donny sang along with his passengers, his voice loud enough to reverberate in his ears. He fancied he could even feel his eardrums vibrating in a pleasingly melodic way as he sang. He liked the feeling, and consequently continued belting out the famous chorus even louder—and with heightening bravado. "Glory, glory, halleluiah, glory, glory, halleluiah, his truth is marching on."

In his music-mind he could not only hear, but also visualize Johnny Cash on stage singing "Mine Eyes Have Seen the Glory," dressed in black, his guitar characteristically hanging from his shoulder, and slung across his back. *What an iconic image,* Donny thought, a smile spreading across his face. That performance was his favorite rendition of his beloved song, and the one now playing loudly on his tour van's CD system. He'd first heard the song as a kid after sneaking into a revival service with a friend.

Among Donny's eclectic selection of music to play—all onboard and at the ready to cater to most tour-group special requests—this Johnny Cash rendition of "Battle Hymn of the Republic" was often requested.

His wife, Delyth, sitting comfortably in the passenger front seat next to him—as she always was—seemed oblivious to everyone's singing. Not a music person, her attention was clearly glued to the book nestled in her lap.

A mystery novel, he guessed, knowing quite well his wife's proclivity when it came to reading material. He kept a pile of secondhand books in the back of the van for their tour groups, many of them mysteries, selected because he guessed Delyth would also like them. Donny also provided copies of the current day's newspapers from the Route 66 towns where he could still find them. The newspapers, his wife usually ignored.

He and Delyth's personalities differed in many ways, but meshed significantly in other respects. Thinking about her while singing—what she liked to read, and how well they "fit" together—Donny felt the corners of his mouth curl into a pleasant-feeling smile. *What a lucky man I am to have Delyth.*

He surely didn't mind her not singing along, for via his oversized rearview mirror—placed perfectly for viewing their van's rear seats without taking his eyes off the road ahead—Donny could see and hear all five of his current high-paying wayfarers fully engaged with belting out "The Battle Hymn of the Republic," with him and Johnny Cash.

"Mine eyes have seen the glory of the coming of the Lord," rang out from front and back of the D&D Tours van.

Also via his mirror, Donny thought they all looked happy, their faces animated, joyous even, as they sang the remainder of the stanza, "His truth is marching on." Indeed, his small travel group finished with a great gusto that brought joy to Donny's singing-soul.

Though their touring van easily accommodated fifteen, he liked small groups like this one—especially when they agreed to pay the full-up rate to have the space to themselves. This particular group was a special club reunion get-together, and they hadn't wanted to share their long anticipated California Route 66 tour with strangers. Of the two women in this small group, the one with the dense mass of dark curly hair piled up high and going-in-all-directions—a Ms. Minor—had made all the arrangements and remitted payment without questioning any fees.

God, do I love t his, Donny thought, and almost expressed his happiness aloud. Indeed, he very much liked all aspects of touring, even cherished what he was doing. Times like this, when not only thinking about—but actually being on the road—he could even feel his heart pound, maybe even skip a beat, then flutter a bit. That feeling of excitement itself, was the best.

Donny brought one hand to his face while keeping his other firmly on the steering wheel. Surprisingly, his cheek felt warm to his touch. He'd expected his skin to be cool from the air conditioning vent pointed his way. He conjectured his heightened excitement and longing for adventure were causing the warmth he felt. *What a morning.*

And when it came to a perfect setting for "excitement and adventure," this morning he was traveling under a clear and beautifully-blue spring sky. There might be a hot desert summer to follow—but right then, the weather was perfect.

Ahh.

Indeed, Donny found being on the road wonderful from many sensual perspectives, including watching the upcoming pavement ahead of him appearing in its unique visual perspective, "feeling" the road below his van as they moved forward, and seeing the miles fading behind him in his rearview mirror.

Although, on occasion during their earlier tour years, the "road ahead" visual perspective had caused Donny to reflexively and hurtfully rub his eyes behind his glasses. *Not anymore.* Thank goodness for surgery and strong glasses several years back.

Thank goodness too, for Delyth's meds. Literally a life saver for her. *That had really scared me.* Donny was really thankful for the advancement in the centuries they lived in. *So much more than Mom had.*

So this morning, instead of going to rub his eyes, his hand instead went to rub his pricey faux Moroccan-leather dashboard. Oddly, it felt unusually cold to his touch, and almost prompted a shiver.

Why these strange temperatures, he wondered? *Was this particular tour group sending out some kind of psychic signals? Something about to happen?* He shook his head. *Silliness,* and he banished such atypical thoughts. Usually grounded in reality, Donny knew it wasn't his beloved tour van giving off a "bad" vibe. *Nonetheless,* he let himself further consider that he'd chauffeured many groups, and each had been different, with its own interpersonal dynamics. Unique, *each and every one.* But none to date had given off "other-worldly" signals. *Silliness for sure.*

He smiled at his goofy thoughts and brought his wandering attention back to driving—for this morning, like it often was on this Mojave Desert section of Interstate 40, there were side-winds buffeting his van. Donny didn't mind—*part of the I-40 experience.* He just needed to keep alert and drive at a modest speed.

And even though he was multi-occupied singing, thinking about the joy of being on the road, driving cautiously, and keeping an eye on his passengers—about half-a-mile back, Donny had *also* managed to notice the sign for the next upcoming exit. Now actually approaching the noticed off-ramp with regret, he slowed considerably, so as to successfully time his leaving the freeway at DAD's exit sign to coordinate with their musical stanza completion.

Once his van was fully on the freeway overpass—and with regret their journey-leg and singing were over—Donny switched off his CD player and turned on his tour-van's intercom.

"Next stop," he said, in a professional and modulated tone of voice, "DAD's RV Park, the first

5

overnight destination on this leg of our tour. And from the campground, if the winds aren't too bad, we'll also be taking a side trip up to that desert castle built by that Gypsy old-timer from Chicago. Been in the news a lot lately."

Then with a genuine enthusiasm he hoped was also reflected in his voice, Donny finished his announcement with a dramatic flurry, "Big adventures ahead."

He wanted to keep their tour exciting, and that castle would be just the ticket, adding to their "Route 66 and more adventure" he and Delyth advertised on their website. For sure, his little group of travelers were paying him good money for this once in a lifetime adventure. And his goal was to give them their money's worth.

A moment passed after his intercom announcement before Delyth actually looked up from her book to peer out her side window. She said softly, more to herself than to Donny, "Looks like we're coming up to DAD's."

Eerily, her words were spoken seconds before Martalina Minor started to scream.

Then immediately after Marta Minor let loose with her ear and mind jolting wails, she next proclaimed in an even heightened volume and intensity, "Anthony's dropped dead! Anthony's dropped dead!"

Early Friday Morning at DAD's before Donny or Leiv Arrived:

"D and D Tours should be pulling in pretty soon," Oliver "Ollie" Llewellyn said. "We have to hurry."

"I know. But we had to first make sure everything was set up for Book Club Friday." Adler "Mack" Wayne's tone mirrored his friend's sense of anticipation and haste. "Takes time."

Mack was DAD's current owner, and the campground's operating-face. And in homage to his now-deceased father's dream and established traditions for DAD's RV Park, he strove for perfection like his father had. Still, Mack was a practical man, and given his campground experience so far, he knew there were always things that needed doing, *or worse*, going wrong. *It was the way of the world, much less our little campground here,* was one of his common refrains. In addition, and unfortunately, he'd also experienced over the five years since his father died — everything always took longer than expected.

"We'll get there, Ollie, not to worry," he reassured his friend and right-hand assistant.

The two men worked well together, and were now jointly draping a gigantic red-and-white checkered tablecloth over several smaller rectangular tables they'd pulled together to form a square near the center of DAD's domed meal pavilion. They had just completed an identical nearby setup for LydiaRose's weekly book club meeting. This setup was for D&D Tours. Per yesterday's phone arrangement with one of the tour company owners, Delyth Latimer, he expected their arrival any moment now.

"The Pavilion" was a spacious, entirely glass-walled, dome-shaped building that served as DAD's multi-use gathering area. There was a much smaller square community laundry room attached on one end of the dome — and on the other end, there was a similar, but more rectangular shaped room-attachment that housed showers, an exercise room, and a modest sauna. From that end's multiuse attachment area, one could proceed to an outdoor pool and lounging area. But even with the shape-modifying end attachments, the main feel of The Pavilion was of a large, open, and spacious dome.

His dad had designed The Pavilion. *His pride and joy,* Mack remembered with a heart-tugging under-his-breath sigh. *Five years already.*

It was the beginning of complimentary breakfast time, and as they worked, Mack noticed in his peripheral vision, that at several tables near the shower room entrance, the group of campers traveling together from Seattle—who had pulled in *en masse* late last night—were already up and eating. From his perspective and distance away in the center of the dome, it looked like they were raring to go, with several in the group holding Route 66 trip guides—and all excitedly commenting back and forth between their tables.

With ideas and preferences, Mack guessed. *Pointing and gesturing, planning their next exciting adventure.* He smiled. *Dad would be happy.* Expecting to be teary-eyed again thinking about his father's dream come true, Mack started a movement to swipe at his actually dry eyes before realizing he had a saltshaker in his hand, and fortunately caught himself in time.

Several other groups of campground-wayfarers he'd checked in yesterday were also up and already eating at various tables scattered around the spacious dome. *Families, friends on adventures together.* A thought he liked.

And all around the dome, a light steam was starting to cover the inside panes. DAD's touted Pavilion breakfast time would soon be in full swing to send them off to their new places—new adventures.

All good.

It was thanks to Josie that aromas abounded. *Olfactory heaven.* Breakfast was Mack's favorite meal. *Just like Dad in that way.* He took a long, deep, aroma-appreciating breath. *Lovely.*

Indeed, "breakfasting" in the pavilion was an amenity his father started during his first week of their ownership. *Fifteen years ago.* And this morning, a new-to-DAD's group of adventurers would be stopping, just in time for breakfast. *Dad would be so proud.* Several other tour groups had stopped in the past, but this was a new outfit — "D&D Tours," their application had read. Mack was definitely looking forward.

Ollie broke into his reverie. "I'm quite sure it's half of the same couple." He spoke with an assurance combined with a surreptitious eye-movement and slight head-gesture directed toward a couple sitting by themselves at a small oval table near the Pavilion's campground grassy area main entrance.

Mack knew Ollie wasn't talking about the anticipated D&D tours, but wasn't positively sure who or what circumstance he was referring to, and said so. "You're talking about the couple sitting near the main door?"

Ollie nodded. "I distinctly remember that huge cowboy hat and those pricey two-tone boots with the swirl engraving the man was wearing. But it's not the same woman." This time he shook his head. "Close, but not her." He shook his head again and tsked.

Now remembering the boots from the previous day himself, Mack said, "Those boots are expensive, I'd guess." He stole another quick look at the couple. "Not surprising we'd remember them."

The stylishly dressed cowboy's face was in shadow from the wide brim of his hat this morning. But that hat, he guessed Stetson for sure, with its pinch-front crease was quite memorable—*definitely an affectation. Then those boots.* Also memorable, yesterday and today.

Something about the woman said "chic and stylish," *probably also a cultivated affectation,* he uncharitably thought. *And carried off quite well.* He visually recalled her name from his campground-register. Della Louise.

"It is curious," he mumbled. But just then, a faint but real gravel-crunching noise pulled his mind away from mental meanderings regarding the cowboy and his wife, his father's accomplishments and wishes, and the dome's aromatic environment.

Out on the campground driveway, next to the line of Pinto palms at the entrance, a van was pulling in.

"Is that the new tour van coming in?" Mack asked and hoped it was. *Or just another "lost in the desert" delivery van using our driveway to complete a U-turn.* An occurrence that happened far more often than Mack would have expected—and occasionally he had needed to give directions. Usually when it was a delivery truck, the driver didn't stop—just completed his U-turn, and headed back toward Shiné Road. But lost travelers usually didn't know where they were out in Mojave Desert land—and he was always glad to help them.

They had completed stretching tablecloths to cover the two tables, and from Ollie's facial expression and body language, smoothed out to his liking. And evidently still in his own thoughts and paying no attention to Mack's tour van question, he said, "I'm telling you," while walking over to Mack's side and half-covering his mouth in a conspiratorial, and forced-casual manner, added, "It's not the same woman."

Mack almost laughed at Ollie's comical spy-type actions, but caught himself in time.

Ollie. In truth, Mack often had to force back a smile when watching his good friend do things around DAD's. A slight man and not tall, Ollie walked with a wee bit of a waddle like a heavier and larger man. He also supported an exaggeratedly long and meticulously cared-for handle bar mustache with large curlicues at the ends. Adding Ollie's baldness and otherwise clean-shaven face into the picture—sometimes Mack couldn't help but smile.

Mack inhaled a slow, deep breath, taking a few seconds to ignore everything else, and refocus on enjoying his favorite combination of smells—freshly brewed coffee, toast, butter, fruity jam, fried eggs—*and cantaloupe today.*

There wasn't much left to do, so salivating slightly, and with added enthusiasm, Mack left Ollie to finish their table preparations alone. He possibly had a van waiting to be checked in, and he needed to do what his father called, "tour the room." He wanted his guests to be "happy-campers," as the saying went. He could almost hear his dad's words of delight—as if he were actually walking with him. *What a life,* Mack thought.

But first, he needed to leave his beloved dome, go outside to the office, and either give directions to a lost sojourner, or check-in a van of new campers.

Chapter Two

Meanwhile at Rhodes Castle

From LC's journal: *Yep, my little room up top is pretty darned fancy for these parts. But I sure love it. And so does little Everett. Me and him like sitting up here a lot in the afternoons, me thinking about stuff, and him building that balsa wood plane Viola ordered him. Sometimes Andre comes too, but he's a morning time kid and likes using his star-map picture right before the sun comes up. Him trying to name them stars without looking at the map thing. Viola ordered him that too, but it only had to come from San Francisco. In Viola's mind, nothings too good for her boys....*

Early Friday Morning: Rhodes Castle Cupola

Intruding into his thoughts as a complete surprise — and seemingly from nowhere — the phrase "Occam's Razor" popped into Leigh-Everett Rhodes's mind. "Where'd that come from?" Leiv asked of his long deceased grandfather across the great divide.

13

He next sighed rather loudly into his grandfather LC's legacy cupola atop Rhodes Castle. Leiv knew he was at yet another crossroad in his life; emotionally, physically, and occupationally. *On all fronts actually.* A crossroad similar to the one he faced when deciding to leave Illinois a few years back. *To return to my childhood home here in Shiné.*

Consequently, Leiv couldn't see why his mind had traveled all the way back to logic classes decades ago in college—even before he was even old enough to drink liquor or vote in Illinois. *No*, he couldn't immediately see a connection to Occam's Razor rule, given the type of revelations he was seeking.

Unless it somehow obliquely, and unconsciously had to do with standing in front of his shelved law and philosophy books in the library downstairs earlier this morning. *The paradigm just mysteriously leaped out at me?* Leiv laughed lightly.

Actually, his whole experience this morning was causing Leiv to feel a tad befuddled and immature on several fronts. And, he certainly didn't think such emotionally confused shenanigans fit with his current age, stature in life, or self-image. *Who* he was, and *what* he was "doing," certainly should have been resolved by this stage of his life. And now, "Occam's Razor" had popped nilly-willy into his consciousness.

Leiv next recalled a conversation several years back with a cousin who was approaching one-hundred years old. At his big birthday bash—his cousin quite vehemently voiced to Leiv his continuing disapproval and regret about several youthful life decisions, and consequent experiences. *Errors in judgment*, Leiv had thought at the time, *surely shouldn't matter any longer.* Yet, the thoughts and emotions

14

from way-back-when, were still banging about in his cousin's brain.

Nonetheless, *even with* that possibly relevant remembrance, and *even with* giving recognition to his own emotional state this morning, Leiv's mind had dredged up William of Ockham's long forgotten construct—*postulating the simplest path was the most probable*—was not at all relevant.

How could it be?

"Isn't, is it? Just more useless claptrap from the past bouncing around inside my brain," he further explained to his grandfather.

Still, and even though the relevance eluded him— Leiv was left with a vague and strangely eerie feeling he couldn't precisely identify, or explain.

He sighed again. This time, louder.

Leiv's current dilemma actually rose to its bothersome status last evening. This morning was a continuation of his feeling of being at a crossroad. In the fading light of dusk, looking for answers and comfort, Leiv had trudged out on a familiar path. Off to his grandfather's secret cave—back around Rhodes Castle, and up the path to LC's private lair.

There, in a darkness Leiv had become comfortable in—maybe even fond of—he sat for more than an hour, clasping his grandfather's journal in his lap. LC's cave was a place and atmosphere where answers had come to him in the past. Leiv was hoping for similar results last night.

Sitting in the cave's eerily quiet and jet-black darkness, ensconced in LC's aged recliner, his own long legs stretched out and crossed at the ankles, Leiv had found himself mulling over how his life had changed since moving to California's Mojave Desert. He let his mind move undirected—for as Leiv knew from past experiences—LC's cave had powers of its own when it came to direction. For sure, his thoughts wandered through his past extensive and eclectic experiences as a judge in Illinois. Experiences which had helped Leiv weather some of the amazing surprises Shiné had presented him with these last couple years.

But real answers had not come to Leiv in LC's cave hideaway.

Now this morning, atop Rhodes Castle, Leiv *still* had his grandfather's diary with him, and with morning light flooding the five-sided cupola—he again hoped for wisdom and answers. Thus, once again holding Leigh Cooper's handwritten words in his hands, but this time with the brightness of another outstanding Shiné sunrise filling all corners of his pentagon-shaped daylight "cave" of sorts, Leiv waited.

And standing there, where he was, as he was, Leiv felt taller than he knew he was. *It's the cupola height and panoramic view,* he thought, *making me feel tall, strong, and capable for a few moments.*

He laughed aloud at himself. *Guidance from the great beyond? Via cave or cupola?* Indeed, Leiv knew himself as a man rooted in reality—except when it came to LC and their communications. And since evening shadows and cave darkness had failed him last night, this morning's hope was Shiné's dawn Mojave landscape—again combined with LC's timeless advice—would somehow now provide the answers he needed.

Yes, this morning, he would make a point to stand in front of the cupola window which provided his favorite Mojave Desert perspective. From this unique cupola spot, out this particular window, Leiv could see all the way to Lookout Loop in the northwest distance. A comforting vista now, given his experiences over the last couple years. In this panorama were also the occasional clumps of Athol trees from here to there—somehow finding water in some underground pockets only the trees knew about. Such clumps had become metaphorical "punctuation marks" in a desert scenery-saga he was still reading.

Thus, this morning—Leiv stood with LC's journal clutched in both hands behind his back, looking out LC's eastern cupola window, his legs slightly spread, with his knees lightly touching the dark-burgundy covered window seat padding, and looking out as far as his gaze took him. Thinking, feeling perplexed, but still emotionally optimistic—he waited.

Leiv even imagined he could smell the early spring morning air he knew covered the landscape before him. Of course, he also knew all cupola windows were closed. In fact, he wasn't sure if they did open. *Don't think I've ever tried any of them.*

Nonetheless, and atypical to his past judicial "facts only" approach to life, Leiv continued to indulge both his real, and imaginary sensory feelings.

Unfortunately, even though his views of Mojave landscape were inspiring and awesome—*nothing* came as he pondered.

Leiv sighed yet again, this time, softly. *My touchstones are failing me.* Not just copula and cave, but his father and grandfather's library, too. For in the wee morning hours before this cupola time, Leiv first started his daytime pondering in their old-world-inspired and memory-laden library—again asking his forebearers for direction from

17

across the years through their library accoutrements. *Standing next to my logic books.* But just like in LC's cave-lair, answers still hadn't come. So, up top he'd gone.

Cave, library, cupola...still no answers...

"I can't even define the problem. Why do I feel at such a crossroads?" *Maybe if I keep speaking aloud, LC will hear?* Leiv almost laughed at himself again. Ironically, he figured Rhodes Castle itself, built by his grandfather and grandmother, with all its physical and emotional portholes to the past, was somehow, and in some way, an important part of this particular crossroads dilemma.

He continued to wait.

Standing where and how he was, with an early Spring dawn fully flooding his Shiné horizon, the sky still sunrise-multicolored—mostly hued with his favorite dreamsycle-colored orange—*surely,* he could talk directly to his forebearers. And answers must *surely* come back to him. *Somehow.*

Alas, instead, yesterday afternoon's time with Glover rehashed itself in his mind's eye.

Leiv sighed yet again.

Through unasked for, and unwanted living-picture remembrances, yesterday quite vividly reappeared to him.

Leiv easily again saw Shiné Police Chief Glover Deers, leaning back in his padded swivel desk chair, staring at his office ceiling and saying, "You never get over seeing stuff like that."

At the time, yesterday afternoon, it was as if Leiv also saw what images haunted Glover as he stared at his office ceiling. And now this morning, even safe and hidden as he was in LC's cupola cocoon, Leiv had to fight back those images, and involuntarily returning images of his own. From yesteryear court proceedings—*earlier times. A different life.*

"Yeah," Leiv had agreed with his friend and half-brother. Glover's tone wasn't actually sorrowful, but yes—*some* emotion had been there. An emotion, Leiv guessed, the Chief of Police would not want revealed to the world. *Not even to me.*

The also present Deputy Walker Johns—part time deputy, ambulance technician, and volunteer firefighter extraordinaire—had also nodded in agreement. Walker was sitting next to Leiv, across the desk from Glover—in what Leiv knew he and Walker both considered harder-than-stone chairs. While Glover, Leiv had often noted during his numerous visits, always had more than adequate pillowing for *his* butt and back in his personal executive-level padded swivel chair.

Chair comfort aside, yesterday afternoon with Glover and Walker had caused Leiv's mind and emotions to dredge up horrendous evidential homicide images from his own experiences. He even remembered numerous lawyers from the old days, on both sides, who unconsciously recoiled and turned their own heads away when introducing such pictures into evidence.

Pictures of head wounds were the worst.

"The only reason they called us in," Glover continued, "was because they're so short of staff, and the poor guy had a Shiné address on an old vehicle registration in his car's glove compartment. It was enough of an excuse to drag me in." The Chief's gaze now lowered from the ceiling, moved past Leiv, out to Main Street via his large storefront-style front window. "Looks like Nate's going home already." Then Glover had looked up at the schoolhouse clock above his office's front door. "It's only three," he added with his trademark click out the side of his mouth. "Wish *I* could go home."

Glover's voice had then taken on a woe-begotten edge to it that Leiv hadn't heard before—causing him to wonder if something else was going on with his friend. Or was it just irritation because he was now involved in a county assist? Leiv asked, "What were the circumstances? Accident, suicide, murder?"

When Glover didn't answer immediately, Walker said, "Chief Deers thinks it's murder." He shook his head. "But San Bernardino Forensics is still calling it an accident." He also clicked out the side of his mouth—a habit he and Leiv had both picked up from Glover. "Something just doesn't seem right though. To me and the Chief."

When Leiv turned sideways to get a better look at Walker, something else in the deputy's face and tone of voice also caught his interest. "What do you mean?" he asked.

"Well...," Walker looked quickly at Glover before continuing—and evidently seeing his talking was okay, said, "I've done some checking for the Chief this morning. Did a lot of computer digging—you know, regarding the victim's finances, business plans, social engagements, that kind of thing. He glanced at Glover again, then said, "And the guy was a racquet ball player, tennis dabbler, swimmer, iron pumper—a real jock type. No way he would have stumbled like that." He clicked out the side of his mouth again. "And I don't think his face should have been that messed up."

Glover said, "It was a set up, I just know it, to make it look like the poor schmuck hit his head on the corner of a table in his living room."

"But you think he was hit? Not an accident."

"Yep. Told the coronor so just a few minutes ago. They're going to keep their eyes out for anything special, or peculiar, or—" His voice broke off and he leaned back in his swivel chair, and again stared at his recently painted light blue ceiling.

"Murder," Leiv had mumbled to himself.

"Are you having your regular shindig thing tomorrow night?" Walker asked with eagerness.

Leiv pulled himself back from revisiting Glover and Walker's County Sheriff assist, and forced his thoughts back to the present and his own dilemma—but then he suddenly realized with a jolt, morning was moving rapidly into full bloom. He had better figure out what was bothering him fast, or forget about further pondering this morning.

Proving, then pushing his point—from his bird-like and panoramic cupola view, Leiv saw Margaret Deers's matador-red Lexus advancing up LC's grand driveway below. He knew she was coming to pick up Adeleine for their bi-weekly book club meeting at DAD's, down at the I-40 junction. Nonetheless, Leiv felt a wee rattle-headed, and surprised at the actual sight of Margaret's car.

"Of course, it's Friday now." *And these last two weeks have flown by.*

Unhampered by reality, but emboldened by self-pity, Leiv returned to bemoaning his "crux in the road" dilemma.

"They have plans, but I don't."

Quickly, Leiv realized he was now wallowing in victimhood—saw it hundreds of times in his courtroom during his judge days. Nonetheless, he indulged himself a bit longer—before finally reaffirming what a pretty darned lucky person he was.

"I just want to feel sorry for myself," Leiv told LC's copula, then smiled and added, "Though it does feel rather nice sometimes, just to wallow."

He also figured another big part of his crossroads issue sprang from his "regal" position as the current overseer of Rhodes Castle in today's world. Of course, he should be the "it" person, given LC was his grandfather—*but still, those damned magazine articles weren't helping.* Nor did the recent newspaper magazine filler and social-media announcements—*appearing all at once out of nowhere*—with tourist-enticing articles, several including helicopter pictures of his grandfather Leigh Cooper Rhodes's iconic "castle in the desert." Even showing the cupola roof right above where he was currently standing.

In defense against all the notoriety, about a month back, Leiv had a fencing crew—under his caretaker Lucca's direction—install a remote-controlled gate at the road entrance. Then Lucca put in chain-link fencing along his Shiné Road frontage to deter the increasing amount of looky-loos.

Winston Moore's daughter—the reason for Margaret Deers's coming by—had appeared on his doorstep with her father last fall. Winston had left and gone back to Illinois.

Adeleine had stayed. Now she was going off to book club with Margaret of all things. *A book club in LC's Shiné!*

An event grandfather couldn't imagine. Well, maybe he could? For sure there were social gatherings of a sort, church events and teas back in LC and Viola's day. *Maybe not so different after all.*

Leiv's cell phone in his jacket pocket rang, startling him out of his reverie.

Once Leiv read who it was, he begrudgingly answered. It was Glover, who immediately said without preamble, even before Leiv could even say hello, "Get hopping. I've been called in by the state and county boys again to assist a second day. Another dead man, down the road at DAD's. I'll pick you up in your driveway. No time to stop and come in and wait for you. You've got about five minutes to get ready. Max."

He looked down, Margaret had evidently picked up Adeleine and just left.

Good grief. And for a second time, the phrase "Occam's razor" flitted through his thoughts as he left LC's iconic cupola and headed downstairs—as he begrudgingly did as bid by Glover.

But once on Rhodes Castle's second floor landing, Leiv straightened his shoulders, blew out a stream of air, and headed for LC and Everett's library—*my library*—so he could tuck his grandfather's diary safely in the wall safe. With a fleeting little smile, Leiv thought back to several years past when Hester *thought* she'd stolen the Mojave Stones from that very safe.

And somehow, that remembrance from initial Rhodes Castle days helped him. For despite current quandaries, circumstances, concerns, and unanswered

23

questions—Leiv's smile and accompanying determination to assist Glover as he had helped him, took the emotional lead.

Chapter Three

Bits and Pieces from Under the Dome

From LC's journal: *When it got dark, we'd have to stop for the night. Never knew what was a waiting for us out there in the night, specially when we reached desert stuff. Remember looking up and a counting stars. It was like we were under a nighttime dome kind of thing. All of us travelers, a thinking our own thoughts. Dreaming our own dreams. Never counted the same number of stars above as the last night. Not never.*

Mid-Friday Morning: Dad's Eating Pavilion – Tables set and occupied

Leiv could hear the distinctive "tire-meets-the-road" hum from Interstate 40. *Just a few miles away.* Significant for him, in that as his unusual morning progressed—*now accompanying Glover and Walker to the scene of another death reported from DAD's campground*—the road-music was an auditory reminder of *all* the people, from *all* across the country traveling on Route 66. As he metaphorically did a few years back. *With all their life stories, ambitions, and desires. Just down the road from my Rhodes Castle.*

The realization that Shiné's isolation in the middle of the Mojave was an outdated fantasy he needed to abandon was unexpected, and it hit Leiv rather hard. Especially, given that the mundane character of "the hum of cars" traveling on the interstate was his mental trigger.

It was also a hard and stark mental flip for Leiv. Since from the very start of his Shiné sojourn, there were indeed, those special nights at the castle when Leiv would sit and take in the night sky outside, and the accompanying evening sounds. In particular, comfortably sitting on his father Everett's teak bench, occasionally he would catch the vague rumblings he thought were either the BNSF, or Union Pacific trains—or cars on the interstate. The same as he was now hearing this morning.

But on those early star-sprinkled evenings, and with his gobsmacked Rhodes Castle perspective at the time— surrounded by his grandfather's trees and his father's bench touchstones—that muted rumble of movement had been comforting. The low hum was a forward-looking harbinger, connecting his ancestors and himself to the current world and fellow human beings. Calming sounds.

Not now, several years later, the humming sound was anything but comforting and "connecting." *No,* more like an awareness wakeup roar. *Millions pass within twenty miles of Shiné every darned day,* Leiv reminded himself, and refrained from sighing aloud.

Instead, he returned his attention to his present reality—the people and circumstances in DAD's Pavilion. Indeed, a dead man, DAD's campground itself, and its owner—Adler "Mack" Wayne—should be leading his thought path.

He had met the fortyish-looking and surprisingly handsome Mack twice before, and guessed him older and more formidable than he initially looked. *Like me,* Leiv teased himself. Their first contact was last fall—for a few moments only—at the big Shiné Community Church meeting held for Shiné enhancement presentations. Then Leiv met Mack once again, recently and for a longer time, giving Leiv the opportunity to actually say hello, and chat a bit. *Right here at this campground.* Although, at that time, Leiv hadn't fully taken in "The Pavilion."

That circumstance was a month or so back. He'd picked up Adeleine from a book club meeting at DAD's. Margaret Deers had taken her to their meeting, but she couldn't bring Adeleine back home—consequently, pickup duty had fallen to him. Leiv couldn't remember exactly why Margaret couldn't bring Adeleine back, but there was something about Margaret needing to hang around longer with a camp resident, LydiaRose. And if he was remembering correctly, Adeleine had explained to Leiv during their drive home, LydiaRose was also called, "The Manchester Woman" by camp residents.

Odd name, Leiv reflected then and again this morning—for someone he guessed wasn't British. But at the time back then, he hadn't asked why the moniker—and this morning, his curiosity quickly evaporated.

However, Leiv did now remember that during his actual chat with Mack a month ago, he'd felt some kind of connection with the man he couldn't explain. *Maybe something to do with forefathers?*

Now, this morning at DAD's with more focused attention and additional conversation, Leiv's initial "forefathers" conjecture-remembrance clarified a bit. Soon after giving directions to Glover and Walker about where the murder van was parked—in an unexpected aside to Leiv—Mack had surprisingly asked him directly about his grandfather Leigh Cooper, and how Leiv liked living there in the castle. Before Leiv could really assimilate what he was being asked, Mack had wistfully added, "I sometimes talk to my dad."

Leiv was so taken by surprise, he didn't immediately know what to say.

Mack next produced an engaging smile accompanied by an introspective turn of the head, before rhetorically asking, "Did I say that out loud?" Then, as if to explain why he'd gone down such a personally direct path with a relatively complete stranger, and with a van holding a dead man only feet away, Mack added with a smile, "I helped my father start DAD's you know."

He considers us kindred spirits, Leiv thought and returned Mack's smile. Couldn't help it. Even with the unexpected personal-like question, he found the man charming. *Charm and good looks. Lucky guy.* Nonetheless, and despite Mack's engaging way, Leiv, hadn't offered very much information about himself, except for the basics of moving from Illinois.

After that exchange, Friday morning moved forward as events took over. And even though Leiv had already interacted with Mack—*possibly one of the main characters under this dome*—it didn't do much to ameliorate his current growing feeling of being dropped in the middle of an unknown soap opera, with a myriad of unfamiliar characters in an otherworldly domed structure.

Truth was, by this point, Leiv's mind was starting to reel from all the new people "dropping" uninvited into his Shiné morning world. He'd started his day in the familiar quiet isolation of LC's cupola "pondering" world—*and now this.*

Suddenly, Leiv felt intensely vulnerable—an emotion he'd seldom had cause to experience—and didn't find pleasant. *Though I've been there before—right here in Shiné land.* Consequently, he further wondered if some unique and newly arrived sense of endangerment was a factor in his crossroads dilemma? *Probably not,* Leiv concluded as he unconsciously rubbed his surprisingly cool forehead—with surprisingly warm fingers.

To counteract whatever was going on within, he quickly put his hands under the table and balled them into fists tight enough to feel his fingernails, then placed his fists on his thighs.

Leiv then returned to straining his brain to encompass all the new names and faces confronting him here in DAD's pavilion. Because for sure, he wanted to help Glover.

Though he wasn't really sure he could. *I know so few of these people.*

Of course, in his past life, he'd had to take in a whole new set of "characters" with every trial. And when it was a high-profile brouhaha—the accompanying media attention pushed him to be knowledgeable fast. But this morning, a few years and a long distance away from the Illinois Court system, he was being sorely challenged. *Age is catching up with me.*

Purposely revisiting the physicality of being in court, Leiv brought his hands up from his lap and placed them flat, face down in front of him, on the checkerboard-tablecloth covered table where he sat between Glover and Walker.

Via flattened hands, Leiv was metaphorically holding on to his courtroom-bench table surface. An oft used habit in those days. He figured this morning, his "hand stuff" was an attempt to physically force his mind and body into perception and understanding mode.

It only partially worked. But he didn't give up. Indeed, Leiv pressed his palms down harder on the tabletop in front of him for a couple minutes more.

Jumping around:

Thus more in control, he thought, and focused on the sights and sounds in his current environment—from his rear and right, Leiv heard, "I know those are the same boots," a man's low voice insisted to fellow book club members around a similar double table behind him.

"And that hat, who could mistake that hat," the man said, completing his thought.

A woman further whispered, "And the new woman with him, hah! Who did she think she was fooling? Not the same. Not the same."

Then Leiv caught an even lower whisper. *Margaret maybe?* "You think he's murdered her?"

Leiv fancied their whispered voices were miraculously carried to his ears by the dome's unique acoustics. A conclusion that caused Leiv to smile slightly at the irony of the book club members whispering in the first place. He also conjectured part of his brain had been purposely trying to eavesdrop without his direct knowledge. Subconsciously, he probably *wanted* to know what was going on with Margaret and Adeleine.

Earlier, after checking out the tour van themselves, then leaving it in SBC Forensics' hands, Glover and Walker were escorted into the Pavilion with him following along. At that time, Leiv had glanced toward the book club table. He didn't actually want to peer at their group, but from that quick look, Leiv thought this morning's gathering consisted of Glover's mother Margaret, his own house guest Adeleine, Mary Jones, incognito Soap Opera Star and owner of Le Bric-à-Brac in Shiné, his former housekeeper Hester Miller-Milhouse, and the now enigmatic, Manchester Woman. There were a couple more women he didn't recognize right off, and one man he didn't think he knew, but wasn't sure. At the time, the tour van inspection and seeing that dead body were prime in his mind—while identifying all the book club members, a side curiosity.

Now seated at the "tour-van" table, to refresh his memory without an obvious peering—Leiv looked back at their table under the guise of supposedly rubbing his brow.

He saw there were actually two men. The man who'd been whispering was the stranger, and to Leiv's amazement, the other man was his friend Douglas "Hermit" Chan.

As for the women, he already knew Hester was a book club member, and realized she was in attendance when he saw Dobie romping and tussling with several other dogs in a large fenced off area viewable from the main office when they first arrived.

Leiv's heart had warmed at the confirmation Dobie was happy and doing well—and for a few seconds, his mind went to Hester, and what a different woman HM "her majesty" seemed to be now. Changing from the scheming gypsy-retributioner when he first arrived at Rhodes Castle, to a now loving and caring doggie-mom. *Dobie must have instinctively recognized she'd have more fun with Hester than me.*

Emotionally, Leiv wouldn't have minded continuing to indulge in early Mojave-Stone memories—thinking about Hester, the Chicago Coopers, Nadya Rhodes Collins, and Sydney Collins—but he pulled himself back, and his thoughts jumped back to Hermit—instead of identifying all the women. Leiv would never have guessed Hermit was in Margaret's book club. *Really gets around for a "hermit."*

Leiv then purposefully lowered his hand from his forehead and turned his head in a way he thought indicated he couldn't possibly be listening to them. Then realizing how silly he was being, turned full-on toward their table for a few seconds, just in time to see Hermit looking right at him with a wry smile.

Can't get anything past that man.

Leiv wanted to sigh, moan, even groan—for he was already finding himself challenged to keep his mind focused on the present, straining to assimilate all the new characters at *his* table, and eavesdrop on the book club table. And all the time, his friend Hermit Chan was mocking him?

Good grief.

* * * * *

The Murder Group:

When they first arrived at DAD's, Mack had immediately explained to the three of them in a down to earth and practical manner, "An Anthony Janus in an arriving tour group dropped dead in their tour van. Hence my call to nine-one-one." *Succinct and comprehensive*, Leiv had thought. Many a time he'd wished for such clarity from defense attorneys and prosecutors alike. Mack added, "One of the women also called him, 'Mr. T,' for some reason."

In the midst of Mack's introductory remarks, his aside with Leiv, and while escorting them to the Mercedes Van scene-of-the-crime parked in front of the campground office—Mack had also squeezed in a quick verbal overarching tour of DAD's—mainly via head movements and finger pointing.

During that time, Leiv also heard the distinctive and very loud wail of an approaching ambulance. *Or the County Coroner's vehicle?* He was still unsure on the "who" point, even though Walker—also a volunteer Shiné ambulance tech himself—had explained several times the incident-decisions dispatchers made.

But Leiv's mind was fully occupied trying to pick up all the pieces of the story about D&D's Route 66 Tours—like *who* these people were, *why* they were stopping at DAD's, and *what* were the circumstances surrounding the death of a passenger right before arrival at the campground?

Was it natural causes? Illness? Or was it murder? Indeed, Mack had mumbled something about a light foam around the dead man's mouth when they pulled in, and the travelers claimed Anthony was clutching at his chest.

Now, in these current moments inside the pavilion, and from his particular position at the "interrogation" table

M.M. Gornell

between Glover and Walker, Leiv could see in detail, not only the tour group travelers, but also aspects of the campground surrounding them he hadn't initially paid much attention to. *Maybe some answers, at last?*

Indeed, where he was sitting—combined with the dome structure itself—offered a panoramic view for him to take it all in. Campground and sojourners. For somehow, under the dome, the *new* players in this *unusual* world, took on larger than life detail. More clarity. More importance.

First a cupola panoramic view early this morning, and now a small-world Pavilion Dome view. But yet again, Leiv's mind detoured—*with past, and present, decision making*—all mentally intertwining. His feeling and view of the world this Friday morning, was again similar to back in his own courtroom in the day.

Back then and there, the olden-style paneled walls framed his special little world. And in turn, "colored" the characters who entered. Sometimes sobering them, but with them still remaining unique players with their own plans, hopes, mental-postures—and sometimes with quite unrealistic dreams.

Leiv shook his head, banishing his past and philosophizing. His thoughts needed to be here and now, in this campground-dome world—versus long gone courtrooms from his past.

A man was dead right now. And one of these people could be a murderer.

Yet, while trying to make himself focus on his own table-group, Leiv couldn't stop himself from again wondering about happenings at the book club table. He wryly supposed they were trying to give the appearance of reading and discussing their book—while actually

34

gossiping in whispers among themselves about strange boots someone was wearing—or maybe what was going on at *his* table. *Nosey as I am,* he figured. Leiv unintentionally turned his head back toward the book club table—and once again, found Hermit staring at him.

Only partially surprised this time, Leiv gave his friend a conspiratorial micro-smile and a wink.

A strobing amber light from the medic-van driving away from DAD's campsite office caught his attention. *Odd,* no siren now accompanied the EMT's pulsing light. Nonetheless, o*ut there in the real world,* the body of a dead man was being hauled off to the coroner—*alive just a couple hours ago.* Most probably, the victim had thought this was going to be a great vacation adventure. Now, he was being hauled off to the Needles morgue.

With a clearing of his throat, Leiv more forcefully commanded his attention to return to the large table where he was sitting—sandwiched between Glover and Walker. To Walker's right, a man whose name he couldn't remember from an earlier introduction, said, "I'm still trying to take it all in."

Glover's investigation needs to take precedence, Leiv demanded of himself, and consequently straightened his back, and honed his attention in on D&D's tour members— and this talking man in particular.

"I couldn't believe what was happening," the man added. Leiv thought he heard disbelief and dismay in his Midwestern-accented voice. An accent Leiv was familiar with from his past in Illinois. "I thought Miss Minor must be joking..." The man quickly lowered his eyes, then amended his statement in a sadder tone while shaking his head, "...not that anyone would joke about something like that."

Leiv now remembered the man's name from their initial introductions—Donny Latimer. Sitting to Donny's right was his wife, Delyth. Together they comprised D&D Tours. And something about them as a married couple, *maybe the way she looks at him,* said to Leiv, "real love." The kind he and Melissa had. *The kind that weathers all storms.*

Delyth. Leiv now recollected being surprised earlier to hear such a solid Welsh name in Shiné—a place which Leiv still considered the "end of the earth." Yet, here he was, sitting in DAD's Campground eating-pavilion, not far from the world renowned Route 66 in the middle of the Mojave—while Glover interrogated a tour group traveling with D&D Tours. *And,* one of the owners was named "Delyth." End of the earth or not, over the last few years, he'd come to realize Shiné definitely had its own special and magnetic aura.

Even though his attention needed to be focused on Donny and Delyth, Leiv's traveling mind jumped yet again, under the guise of wanting to see how Adeleine was faring, so for a few seconds once more, Leiv stole yet another glance at the Book Club table. *Competing pulls, emotions and logical thought.* For sure, his feelings about Adeleine were also puzzle pieces in his crossroads pondering.

Not now. Leiv pulled himself back to the tour group.

Donny rubbed his eyes behind his glasses and continued, "Nothing like this has ever happened on one of our tours...," his voice caught a tad, "...I've never even been that close to a dead body." Donny next described their trip itinerary and amenities—starting with the logistics and mechanics of gathering them all together at Santa Monica Pier.

His explanation, Leiv thought, *told in over-dramatized detail.* Nonetheless, Donny's recitation, maybe because of all the elaborate detail, sounded genuine to his ear. And Leiv thought his own sixth sense well-trained to spot sincere-sounding scoundrels. A lot of "scoundrels" had paraded themselves through his courtroom over the years. Leiv caught himself mid-reminiscence, and was able to refrain from going farther down yet another memory-lane tangent.

"We planned on stopping here at DAD's from the start," Donny, was explaining, "and I figured Mr. Wayne could set us up for today and tomorrow after I explained to him where and what we wanted to go and do...."

Leiv certainly could understand the appeal of a tour overnighting here at DAD's right off Route 66—but he wasn't quite sure why they'd stop here in the morning like this. There was Ludlow just a little farther down I-40, or just a small detour down to Amboy, or even Needles, with a side trip to Laughlin—all within just a couple hours range farther.

Donny answered Leiv's mental question as soon as he thought it. "It's perfect for a morning base stop. We can shower, eat breakfast, then head on up to Kelso or Nipton, or this new attraction, some kind of castle in the desert, the one that's been in the papers recently."

Leiv was barely able to hold back a stage-level gasp, while looking to Glover, who was playing at ignoring him, while continuing to look past him and Walker at Donny. Leiv did think he caught a sliver of a smile, or maybe it was a twitch, curling the corner of the Chief's mouth. Walker, though, was turned directly toward Leiv, and openly smiled at him. Leiv clamped his mouth shut.

His thoughts, however, were not pleasant.

More revelations under the dome:

Donny's wife was next—and as if she were talking about some mundane everyday occurrence in life, not a murdered man found in their Mercedes van—Delyth, adding to her husband's comments, said, "We loved this dome from an earlier visit, and their breakfast was really good. Not what you'd expect at a campground."

True enough, the place does have a nice "feel" to it," Leiv admitted. *And it does smell really good.* Indeed, the aromas of bacon, toast, coffee—all floated through the open dome space. *An apt situation to use the word "wafted,"* he mused, while slipping back down the memories-path for a moment—re-seeing the actual page of a legal brief wherein a lawyer unbelievably used the word "wafting" to describe the decomposition odor at a crime scene.

His memory and Delyth's observation aside, Leiv doubted any food at DAD's—no matter how good their breakfast menu might be, or the aromas he was currently taking in—could come close to matching The Greasy Spoon. Chef Jack and his TGS restaurant, next to Shiné Pump and Fill, were now at legendary status in Leiv's mind and heart.

However, given Delyth's words of praise, Leiv wondered why he hadn't tried eating at DAD's before? Especially since he knew about The Pavilion from Margaret and Adeleine each talking about their book club. Leiv even knew from their laudatory remarks, Josie was the cook's name; and he resolved to try her breakfast offerings for himself sometime in the future.

I've mentally wandered again. In trying to stop his mental hijinks, Leiv was surprised with an unexpected community-disconnect feeling, quite similar to his experience last summer at the Shiné Community Church proposal gathering. Once again, he was being confronted with what his grandfather's Shiné world now actually encompassed.

So much has happened since I first had to deal with Mojave Stones, Hester, the Chicago Coopers, Mary Jones, Margaret Deers, and finding out about Glover's connection to me.

This time, Leiv was able to force his attention back to their table, even though he also heard intriguing noises behind his back—and even with his current resolve— wanted to turn around and check out the Book Club table again. He didn't.

Just a few feet away around his table, and sitting next to Delyth, Marta Minor was saying "I'm sorry I screamed so loud. But like Mr. Latimer, I've never seen a dead body before...at least anyplace outside a funeral parlor...or at a wake." Her tone softened a bit, "Actually, I wasn't sure he was dead until I unbuckled my seat belt and went to him." Then her voice caught a bit. "But the way he looked...not moving or anything. I just knew he was dead." She gasped, before adding, "And there was foam around his mouth...." Her voice faded to silence.

Unbelievable to him, Leiv's mind wanted to wander down memory-lane yet again, so this time he took a long, slow, and deep breath—as surreptitiously as he could by placing his hand across his face, shielding both his nostrils and mouth. Internally, he was getting sorely irritated at his inability to focus and control his wandering mind. Not only in current time—but also last night in LC's secret cave, and earlier today in both Rhodes Castle's library and LC's cupola this morning. With building irritation, Leiv chided himself, *I'm too old for this past memory crap. My past is history.*

Eventually and slowly, he let his deep breath back out, but this time under the guise of rubbing his eyes. Leiv's deep breathing was meant to calm, re-center, refocus his attention.

He reminded himself, *a man has dropped dead in a tour van on the way to a campground.* Leiv let his head drop back slightly so he could look at the pavilion's domed ceiling—taking in a beautiful Shiné morning sky through slightly-steamed domed glass triangles. For sure, he could still make out reds, oranges, yellows—but now as morning had progressed, all colors were melding and seemingly floating across an unusually cerulean blue Shiné sky.

With that simple act of appreciating yet again, his Shiné morning—along with taking in and out his slow deep breath—Leiv felt better. Back in control of his thoughts, he hoped. But still reaffirming his earlier observation, *that Delyth lady is right.* Even with Glover's murder investigation going on, and a whispered intrigue about some man's fancy boots—there was an oddly compelling "feel" to this pavilion dome.

It wasn't something he could precisely articulate. But the way the tables were set all around, the size of the place, not too small or too large, the expansive height of the dome, the shape of the glass panels—and the aromas. Not just the breakfast aromas, but there was also that unique smell Leiv had noticed before in other circumstances. *The desert.*

Somehow the Mojave was able to invade inside the dome. *With its own sweet smell.* Mrs. Delyth Latimer must have picked up on it, too. *Interesting woman,* he thought vaguely. *Sensitive. Intuitive.*

Melissa had been like that too. Feeling a place. Quickly he banished thoughts of his deceased wife. *So much for my breathing exercise.*

"I'm not surprised he's dead," a lady next to Marta Minor and almost directly across the table from Leiv said. "Many a time I could have killed him myself!" She made a disparaging sucking sound through her teeth. "But the fact one of us actually did it is—well it's amazing."

Regardless of her words, Leiv was sure the expression he read on her face was one of approval. Indeed, her expression said, *a good deed, done well.*

"And your name is Gillian Butté?" Glover confirmed in a calmer voice than her bombshell statement should have evoked. He did look down for a couple seconds at a piece of paper on the table in front of him.

"Gill," she said.

"And it's your statement—Gill—that Anthony Janus's death was murder, and not a surprise to you?"

Gill nodded her head vigorously. "I almost didn't come. Right, Marta?"

Marta nodded a somber-looking acknowledgement.

Tom Carter, another member of the tour group and next in line around the table said, "Still, Gill, that's a rather harsh thing to say. You know we all wanted to come. You didn't dislike Tony that much, did you? And I think he had a heart attack." Tom had a distinctive salt and pepper beard.

Leiv thought the censure he heard in the otherwise rather plain-looking, slightly portly-faced, middle-aged man's voice was rote, rather than from genuine conviction or concern. He was saying what was expected—not necessarily how he felt.

Well, Anthony wasn't universally liked, it seems.

In an effort to really understand what was going on, especially with his disconnected attention-focus this morning, Leiv started by first reviewing the tour group members in his head. Trying to fix them with their names, putting everyone in a mental cubbyhole of sorts. He guessed Glover had been doing that himself, but he was supposed to be helping his friend.

In his past life, he'd developed a little pigeon-holing mental ID-ing thing, complete with cages with little name plates on the front of their pigeon doors. He'd developed his little game of sorts, during a horrendously long, tedious, and multi-character swindling ring case. *A long time ago down memory-lane again.* Leiv recognized one of this morning's "pigeons," sitting at this very table in their little "character-pigeon-cages," could be a murderer.

Of course, Anthony's death *could* have been caused by an allergy, or some kind of stomach condition. Or, as Tom Carter suggested, a heart attack. However, though trying to be creative when it came to life's hazards, not many other causes of death, other than murder, were immediately jumping out at him. Leiv wanted to know why this Gill lady thought Anthony had been murdered. And then how? And of course, who?

Leiv began checking off the names—*one*, Anthony "Mister T" Janus, the deceased. Tour member number two, Martalina "Marta" Minor, the screamer, was at this table, sitting next to tour member number three, Gillian "Gill" Butté, who was sitting directly across the table from him. Finally, there was Tom "Z Man" Carter. *That's only four?* Leiv was sure he'd heard earlier it was a five-person tour.

Indeed, with all his mental jumping around this morning, Leiv questioned his observational faculties. *Have I missed a piece of the action?* Where was number five? *And why,* he snidely mused, *do all these people use nicknames at their age?*

Admittedly, from the glimpse he'd gotten of "Mr. T" Anthony Janus's corpse earlier, he was clearly a body-builder, even into middle-age—thus his nickname, which might have been quite appropriate in his earlier life—had remained valid, even now. *In death.*

Just as Leiv was finally coming to terms with assimilating the D&D Tours participant's information, and hope for the Chief to now zone in on possible murder details, Glover's cell phone rang. Shiné's chief of police looked at his phone's face with an irritable expression as if to decline the call—instead, he abruptly stood up walked a couple feet away and turned his back on everyone.

For several moments, the attention of all table members was focused on Glover's back as he first nodded, then mumbled some words that sounded to Leiv like "okay" and "got it."

When he turned back to all of them, Glover smiled as if nothing out of the ordinary had happened, came back and sat down in his chair, and continued, "Sorry for the interruption." His voice sounded like the call had been a non-issue. "I need to verify what I have here is correct. You have all filled out the forms I gave you completely with your names and addresses for our records?" He tapped the papers on the table in front of him.

Nods around the table. Leiv watched as Glover took them in one by one.

The Chief looked around the table slowly, including taking Leiv and Deputy Walker in his somehow commanding visual sweep, then said, "Forensics are still working on your van, as you can see outside the dome." Robotic nods again. "They will also be taking finger prints from all of you, and possibly taking DNA samples if they come up with anything in the van that needs matching to." Nods from all again, no pushback from any of them. "For right now, let me read what I have here back to you. Then I'm sure Mr. Wayne and staff will get you coffee or whatever you'd like."

Leiv thought coffee and breakfast were not a high priority on any of their lists. *How Anthony died is.* Leiv also knew, that seeing dead bodies up close and personal, hit most people hard—though in different ways—but for sure, the experience never was an appetite stimulant. No matter how good Josie's food was.

Using his notes, Glover began summarizing his interviews so far, officiously for sure, but Leiv thought more hurriedly than was his usual style—and stating Gill's thought about murder as just another ordinary piece of information.

Again, Leiv heard a muted siren wail fading into the distance. *The body bag containing Anthony "Mister T" Janus on its way to the coroner?*

Then before Leiv could catch on, or catch up, Glover gathered his papers, stood up, nodded to Walker, and they both left without further ado. Neither man said a word to

Leiv before turning toward the main pavilion door and heading out.

Annoyed they hadn't spoken to, or included him, Leiv stood up himself, but turned to his rear, and went to sit in an empty chair at the book club table next to Adeleine. *Hell with both of you.*

Even more revelations under the dome:

"Is this seat taken?" he asked his houseguest, Adeleine—and by now, a friend.

"Yeah, but even when she comes back, LydiaRose won't mind moving over one so you can slide in."

It seemed like within seconds of sitting down in the seat offered by Adeleine, Leiv felt a hand on his shoulder and looked up into the face of LydiaRose, "The Manchester Woman."

She looked directly into Leiv's eyes and said, "I bet you want to know about the boots, right?"

Leiv was greatly taken aback by a feeling of being overwhelmed. *Why?* Not something he'd felt for many a year as a much younger man.

On automatic pilot, he stood and pulled over another chair for The Manchester Woman. But before Leiv's thoughts and body could connect—much less understand—what was emanating from this woman, Walker Johns was at his side.

"We're waiting for you in the patrol car," Walker announced rather peevishly. "What's taking you so long?"

"I thought..." Leiv started.

Walker cut him off. "You know he likes you tagging along." Then Walker smiled teasingly. "Let's go."

As they were leaving, a California Highway Patrol cruiser was pulling in and parking in front of the campground office, and Walker answered Leiv's non-verbalized question. "CHP is assisting *our* assist to the County. Keeping an eye on our little merry band of travelers while we're gone. Making sure no one goes anywhere but DAD's. If Anthony Janus's death is determined murder, we want to know where that little tour group is. 'Cause one of them is the murderer."

Chapter Four

In a Nutshell

From LC's journal: *Have to tell, sometimes I was a scared on the road heading west. Remembering I had to look somewhere else excepting that trail when I was coming through that pass. Black Mountains I'm remembering...and them desert sections...for miles and miles...*

Leiv had ridden with Glover in his Shiné Police cruiser on the freeway several times before—both alone, and with others. Consequently, he figured he should be accustomed to sitting in the backseat like a perp, with the cruiser's strobe light revolving, and Glover lead-footing-it—while simultaneously maneuvering back and forth through interstate traffic like he was on an incident-callout. Trucks, cars...it seemingly didn't make any difference to Glover.

But much to the contrary of being at ease, Leiv still hadn't come to terms with his friend's driving. Glover's weaving in and out on the interstate at eighty-plus miles an hour, while vying for open lane space with aggressive southern California drivers—was still unnerving. *Scary even.*

Nothing like the experiences from Leiv's past Illinois police ride-a-longs. *Of course, they were on their best behavior with me in the cruiser.* Again, Glover, clearly didn't feel any such behavior constraints.

And since Leiv wanted to be "in on the action" — especially since Glover was increasingly including him — he put his *metaphorical* head in the sand, and tried to keep his *physical* head bent forward with his eyes on the stack of papers in his lap — Glover's notes on the D&D tour group.

"I'm going to be really surprised if Coroner Jack comes back with 'natural causes' like a heart attack or something." Glover was speaking to his part-time deputy, Walker Johns, sitting in the passenger seat next to him, but talking loud enough for Leiv to hear.

"Me too," Walker agreed. "I bet you a breakfast at TGS that it's murder."

"Nope. You're not suckering me in."

Leiv peeked up from his lap enough to see Glover shake his head and add, "Not betting against something I agree with."

He smiled to himself, but didn't look up any further. *Eyes down, eyes down.* Leiv knew a breakfast-payout was a teasing-level sore point between the two men — in that Glover had humored Walker by accepting his bets in the past — and consequently, ended up paying for several breakfasts at TGS. Indeed, Walker was often right. And savvy enough to know when to bet. Or not.

When first heading out from DAD's on this business "road trip" for an interview, Leiv's rash — and probably unattainable plan — was not to look around until Glover arrived in Barstow. *Most probably impossible,* he guessed from the start.

True enough, it was turning into a beautiful clear mid-morning, with a high seventy-degree temperature to match. Thus, after five more minutes or so, and craving to see the passing scenery, Leiv finally looked up—*but only out my window*, he rationalized. As expected and as desired— golden rolling stretches of scrub desert—touched by the brilliance of full-in-the-sky sun greeted him. Cactus, creosote, and dirt roads to nowhere...brilliantly illuminated.

In that moment, it came to Leiv—the resolution to his crossroads dilemma. His "dilemma" was no "dilemma" at all.

A manufactured crisis that I can only resolve by running away once again.

But *no*, he didn't want to actually leave Shiné, return to a world he *thought* about a lot, but no longer *cared* about. His past was a much-changed world he wasn't sure he even wanted to adapt to.

No, Shiné was where he wanted to be. And solving this case with Glover and Walker is what he wanted to do. So, stepping heartedly into his Shiné world, Leiv fully and resolutely lifted his head and said loud enough for both Glover and Walker to hear him, "Have I read correctly...these travel group people have known each other from grammar school?"

Glover nodded, and Walker actually spoke, "Yep." Then after a headshake and a Glover style mouth click, added "Can't imagine still being friends with some of the people I went to grammar school with."

"So this wasn't just a from 'back in the day' reunion kind of thing, but also a 'friendship despite the years' kind of confirmation thing?" Leiv tried to clarify.

Glover and Walker both nodded.

Leiv added, "I got the impression Gill and Tom weren't that enthused to rekindle their friendship with Anthony Janus." Then he turned his head back to look out his window at the Mojave along I-40 again. They were passing through one of his favorite stretches around Newberry Springs, and soon—if they were lucky and had a few spring rains—the center-strip would be full of small desert wildflowers.

"When Anthony gagged," Leiv continued with an emotional enthusiasm that surprised him, "he foamed at the mouth a bit, then fell forward, right? And Donny Latimer was driving, and Delyth was sitting next to him happily reading a mystery."

Leiv paused a moment, before further pulling together everything he'd just read into a coherent verbal retelling. "Marta Minor was sitting on the bench kind of seat across from Anthony, while Gillian "Gill" Butté was sitting to Marta's right, also across from 'Tony.'" He took a breath, closed his eyes and let his head drop back a bit, trying to better visualize the group arrangement inside the murder van. "And Tom 'Z Man' Carter was to Marta's left in the van, also across from Anthony."

"Yep," Walker confirmed.

"And the fifth tour member we haven't met yet?"

Once more, Glover nodded.

"He was taken straight off to Barstow Hospital, and that's where we're going now."

Again, nods from Glover and Walker.

"Why? What's wrong with him? I didn't see it in your notes..."

Walker did the explaining. "He was sitting next to Anthony, and when Anthony fell forward, it knocked the cooler in the tiny space between the two benches with all the cold ice all over Tim 'Backup' Frasier, causing Mr. Frasier to jump straight up and hit his head on the van ceiling. A lot of blood from what I hear, but he said he was okay. But the EMT dispatcher insisted they also send an ambulance to take him to the hospital."

Leiv thought back to sitting in the dome. "I *was* hearing the sirens of two ambulances...." He looked down at Glover's notes again. "The group member Tim 'Backup' Frasier." He sighed slightly. "Hate having to keep the names Tom and Tim straight." Though in this case, Tom "Z Man" Carter's distinctive beard and portly build would help Leiv at least visualize the "Tom," in the Tom-and-Tim set. Still, he was yet to meet Tim "Backup" Frasier— hopefully he would have distinctive characteristics. "And all these nicknames—"

"Goes back to grammar school stuff I think," Walker said.

"You're probably right," Leiv agreed. "Any nickname offered for the victim?"

"'Mr. T,'" from Walker again. "And Tony, which I think is commonly short for Anthony."

"Oh yeah, right. I knew that." Leiv's mind flitted back to a memory of a DA way back when, who kept calling the accused Tom, when his name was Tim. To this day, Leiv thought that name confusion had caused the DA to lose his prosecution that day. "And this Tim Frasier guy was sitting next to Anthony in the van?"

"Yep."

51

"And before Tim Frasier jumped up and bashed his head, Anthony had just keeled over after several swallows of some special soda they all liked and had requested D&D Tours to provide. Then Marta Minor screamed."

Leiv filled, then blew out cheeks full of air before continuing. "And those sodas were in a cooler right in front of them the whole time from Santa Monica Pier." He allowed himself to look outside their fast-moving cruiser long enough to see Glover pull out and proceed to pass what looked like a four semi-truck caravan. Quickly he averted his eyes, and turned his head back to the notes in his lap.

"Well, your forensics report is going to tell you a lot. Especially on the cooler contents. And Anthony's stomach contents...." Not having ever visited the coroner's office, Leiv's mind pictured TV generated type images of Coroner Jack and his crew combing the inside of D&D's luxury Mercedes tour van—digging into its luxury padded seats, vacuuming the van's thickly carpeted floor, and swabbing its expansive vista-viewing windows.

In contrast, Leiv next visualized that same van *before* ending up with the coroner—with five happy passengers. And Donny pleasantly driving along I-40, almost at his DAD's destination, and all singing the same song—*Battle Hymn of the Republic*. He wondered if Delyth had joined in with the final chorus, or continued reading her book as stated in Glover's notes. *Then death had struck.*

Leiv clicked out the side of his mouth, Glover-style—but with minimal sound.

* * * * *

"I'm surprised somebody hadn't killed the bastard already," Tim "Backup" Frasier said in an incongruously weak and pathetic tone.

Another Anthony Janus fan, Leiv mused.

He had turned from the thin man laying in a ubiquitous-looking hospital bed—with all the equally ubiquitous-looking ICU tubes and bottles connected to digital displays—and walked over to Tim's hospital room window. There he stood, hands clasped behind his back—listening.

"Tony Janus was a mean bully type." Tim coughed weakly. "All his life. From grammar school on..." His voice weakened even more. "But he had something that attracted people...well us kids at least."

"Take your time, Mr. Frasier. We're just glad you could talk to us." Glover was sitting by his bed, pulled up real close. Leiv knew he wanted to get as much information as possible—not miss anything—without pushing the edges of decency.

Quiet hung for several long moments.

And as Leiv looked out one of Barstow Hospital's still newish windows—out and on to Main Street Barstow—recent memories returned. Ones Leiv surely would never like to relive. There was Twenty-Nine Palms Logistics Base hospital several years back with Glover—and then just this last fall at this very Barstow Hospital with his caretaker Lucca Fabero in a similar bed.

And here he was once more, front and center, having to choke down distasteful hospital trappings and the illnesses of others. For a moment, along with his distaste, Leiv was awash in an intense love for LC, while thinking about what a different world he lived in from his grandfather.

No hospitals like this back then. Indeed, he thought yet again, about what a remarkable man LC must have been.

"I never liked him." Tim was talking again.

Glover pushed, "But you still hung around him. And went on a tour here with him decades later."

Leiv turned back to the hospital room scene in time to see a minute smile of pleasure cross Tim Frasier's face.

"Where Gillian goes, I go."

Few words, but they told a long story of unreciprocated love—maybe adoration even—spanning decades. *Motive for murder maybe?*

Seemingly reading Leiv's mind, Tim added ever so softly, "But I didn't kill him."

Again, the room was quiet for a bit. He, Glover, and Walker, waiting. Thinking.

Finally marshalling enough strength, Tim added, "I should have. Killed him, that is. Years ago. Too much of a coward."

The hospital room door opened, and a small man, with a voice of authority laced with displeasure, stated quite forcibly, "I'm Dr. Hari, and I gave strict instructions this man is too ill to talk to anyone." Dr. Hari had a stethoscope around his neck, and a clipboard in his hand— and next gave them all the evil-eye as he scanned the room.

Leiv followed meekly as Glover and Walker led the way out of Tim Carter's room.

For some inexplicable reason, in passing, Leiv winked at Dr. Hari. He received a smile in return.

Chapter Five

Back on the Home Front

From LC's journal: *One place I stopped was a farm where they fed people heading west for a little money. None of us had much to pay them anyways. I remember to this day the big sign they had out front. "All Welcome." What I remember most was the daughter. Her name was Viola. She is my heart. My everything I do think.*

What a long morning. Leiv was tired, but not too tired for Adeleine.

Especially since they'd both headed back to Rhodes Castle kitchen fairly close in time. Her from DAD's via a lift from Margaret first—and Leiv, dropped off by Glover on their way back from Barstow a little later. And his kitchen now—unlike the cold unwelcoming part of the house when it was Hester Miller running things—"HM's kitchen" had transformed into a warm and welcoming spot in the castle.

All Adeleine's doing.

Rhodes Castle kitchen was now a place where they could actually talk while eating. An added bonus—Winston Moore's daughter was turning out to be a discerning cook.

"The Manchester Woman thinks you're handsome," Adeleine said, while finishing up arranging a tea-serving tray at the kitchen counter holding Hester's stainless steel double sink. "I kind of think she has a crush on you."

Sitting at the large round kitchen table behind her, Leiv humphed dismissively, and thought, *a "crush?" What an old-fashioned word.* His ego did lead him to wonder if Adeleine was speaking the truth? *Or,* maybe even speaking for herself? He certainly hoped not—in either case. Melissa was the one and only love of his life.

"She even asked me what type of books you read and what kind of music you like?" Adeleine chuckled as she turned from the kitchen counter and headed Leiv's way. "And she asked me what was your favorite ice cream flavor."

Leiv was caught off guard, and didn't have a ready excuse not to answer. So he quipped, "Sounds like she wants to do some kind of psychic reading." Then on quick second thought, he decided Adeleine deserved a decent answer, not a smart-alecky retort. So, he added in a considered tone, "Non-fiction history, Baroque, and chocolate."

"And she says you're the kind of man who takes on a different look to different people."

"Not sure I know what you're talking about..."

"Good height and handsome to some—shorter, serious and sturdy to others. Father always thought you looked intellectual, especially when you were sitting on the bench."

He was sure he didn't have a clue to what Adeleine was saying about his looks. His height and weight never changed. And as far as he knew, his demeanor was pretty constant.

"The thing is," Adeleine said as she finally arrived behind Leiv at the huge table, "his boots were quite extraordinary. And that hat…it was gigantic."

Leiv laughed outright at both the disconnect between Adeleine's statements about his looks and the cowboy couple speculation—and the knowledge he'd followed her thought pattern without a hitch.

With bringing his mind back to the mysterious campground couple, the hat part once again reminded Leiv of a case he'd presided over—way-back-when in Night Court. *Feels like a hundred years ago now.* The case had moved up to a higher court on his recommendation, but the initial Night Court incident involved a bar shooting in a small Illinois farming town, where one drunk store clerk insulted a drunk ranch-hand's hat. Leiv had learned more about cowboy hats and gear during that case than he ever wanted, or figured he needed to know. *Ever.* Yet, here he was, talking cowboy hats and boots with Judge Winston Moore's daughter in his grandparent's huge kitchen.

"Funny how things turn out," Leiv said aloud in response to his remembrance. "Probably a Stetson Cattleman from the glimpse I got." Truth was, he'd snuck a couple more glances earlier when still in the dome, and he vaguely re-visualized a wide-brimmed cowboy-styled hat, light tan in color, and with a dark brown hatband. "Don't know much about boots, though, but those sure looked custom. With all the fancy scroll work...." His voice trailed off. Leiv now regretted he hadn't looked closer before being rushed out of the dome by Walker.

"This is a mixture of Scottish breakfast tea, Yorkshire Gold, and a bag of Constant Comment." Adeleine set down the large teapot-laden tray into the space in front of Leiv. Then she walked around the table and sat down directly across from him. "Ollie did say the name of the boots, said they were expensive, but I forget what he called them. I think it was a person's name, maybe?"

Hester's legacy table was a large oval, and in the past, ill suited for being intimate enough to feel connected. But now sitting across from Adeleine, he felt quite in tune with her.

Hester.

Table size aside, in current time, Leiv found himself appreciating Hester's innate savviness. In fact, during several thoughtful times since her marriage to the set-designer, David Milhouse, last year—Leiv even regretted some uncharitable thoughts he'd harbored in the past. *Only occasionally,* in that it was hard to forget, much less forgive her constant scheming to steal his grandfather's Mojave Stones.

"I think you might like it," Adeleine said pouring Leiv a mug full of tea. "I gather you did see them in the dome...at the table to your right near the entrance to the showers and stuff?"

"Yes, but not close enough to really look...and I was hurrying. But even at a quick glance, they really were quite a couple alright. Though I don't know much about western gear, those boots had to be handmade. By a real craftsman I would guess."

Leiv knew he was becoming fond of seeing Adeleine's smiling face across the table from him—especially during the meals they shared together. Even though he often still headed down to TGS for breakfast with Glover.

"Oh," she said jumping back up. "I forgot the donuts."

"Donuts?"

"Margaret and I picked them up at TGS when we went into Shiné yesterday to check out Nate's Bookstore. I put them in the freezer, then took them out this morning. They're in the microwave now."

Leiv had yet to check out the interior of the new bookstore himself. Just looked at his storefront across Main Street from Shiné Police office, and speculated with Glover about the store's owner. And like with Mack Wayne at DAD's, Leiv had also met Nate once at the meeting about proposals for Shiné projects.

In line with Leiv's Shiné-project-memory-chain-of-thought, after a moment, he mused aloud more to himself than Adeleine, "You know, Hermit Chan is still talking about building a camera obscura."

Adeleine, returning from her quick trip to the microwave, and carrying a greasy paper bag in her hand, was already back close enough to the table to hear him. "I bet you were thinking about the bookstore, then that crazy meeting about new projects, then Hermit's proposal."

Amazing. Melissa used to read his mind like that—understand the ways his mental wanderings went. Quickly, he pulled back from such thoughts.

"Yep," he agreed with a lighthearted laugh. He looked down at his mug. "This tea smells great."

Adeleine commenced removing and arranging her bagged donuts on a small serving plate already sitting on the table.

The sight and smell of the grease-laden raised donuts covered in drizzled simple sugar icing caused Leiv to instantly salivate. *How can I possibly still remember that corner bakery in Springfield? And how could Chef Jack know?*

"I've had one," she said through a resigned sigh. "And it's taken all the restraint I have not to eat the whole bag." She licked her lips, then on the tea front, squeezed a few drops from a lemon wedge into both her and Leiv's mugs.

Then Adeleine proceeded to retell to Leiv, in picturesque detail, how this couple appeared at DAD's, with his distinctive hat, top of the market cowboy boots, and a stunner of a wife on his arm several days ago. Then he reappeared this morning with a wife that was not quite the same. "At least that's what Ollie, and Mack, and The Manchester Woman, and Josie think."

"And you?"

"I wasn't there when they first arrived. Just there this morning. Ollie swears the woman doesn't look the same."

Leiv then proceeded to fill her in on what Tim "Backup" Frasier told them at Barstow Hospital.

Adeleine and I are confidants, he thought. *Nice.*

Nonetheless, accompanied with an under-his-breath sigh, Leiv found himself bemoaning, *What a long day. And it isn't over yet.*

* * * * *

Not quite several hours later, rather proud of himself for having inside information on the cowboy couple, Leiv decided to keep his big reveal about the change of wife circumstance at DAD's to himself until the perfect moment. Besides, he wanted to hear all the latest on the tour-van murder first.

"Cardiac glycosides," Needles Deputy Sheriff Brad Temper said as he deftly slid the report across the mirror-polished TGS's back booth tabletop and into Glover's waiting hands. "I tried bringing it to your office, but the front door was locked with your 'Call 911' sign hanging in the door window. And your cell kept going to message...."

Leiv was sitting to Brad's left, and even though tired, was enjoying the atmosphere, anonymity, and cop fellowship the back booth at TGS's provided. And he certainly didn't want to miss anything. However, he wasn't able to glean anything from the ubiquitous manila folder as it journeyed from the Needles Deputy hands, across the tabletop to Shiné's Chief of Police. Reining his curiosity in, Leiv waited.

"We were at Barstow hospital," Glover explained to Brad, "and I had my phone going to messaging." He cleared his throat and opened the folder. "That's why I knew to call you back and ask you to meet us here."

Indeed, Glover had dropped Leiv at Rhodes Castle, then had also called him within half an hour after arriving back at his police office with this invite. And now, Leiv, Brad, Walker, and Glover were all enjoying heavenly aromas coming their way from Chef Jack's kitchen. From Jack's side, when they arrived, he would only say their late-afternoon meal would be a surprise.

They were sitting only feet away from the kitchen

door—but Leiv couldn't identify what his favorite chef was cooking up—but definitely thought Glover's recommendation to come into town to TGS's, had been excellent. And even though Leiv had just enjoyed delicious donuts with Adeleine less than an hour ago, he still heard minor hunger-rumblings in his stomach—and felt hunger pangs starting to build. *It's the aromas.*

Sitting next to Glover across the booth table from Leiv and Brad, Deputy Walker Johns looked over at the folder his boss was starting to go through. "Any indication in there Anthony had heart rhythm problems causing him to need a heart drug?" Walker paused, but before Glover could answer, he added, "What I mean is, except for that awful look on his face, his body certainly looked fit. Worked out a lot."

Glover's attention was on the contents of the manila folder—but across the table from him, Brad nodded in an empathetic manner. Leiv thought he might have nodded a bit himself—but wasn't sure. Regardless, there was no one to see or hear them. Front and back were empty except for them.

TGS was next door to the town's only gas station—Shiné Pump and Fill—and the restaurant was seldom full. Neither was it seldom completely empty. Chef Jack officially opened the restaurant part at six in the morning, and closed his kitchen around eight in the evening—a couple hours after his wife Becca opened the attached tavern around six. Limited bar-food was consequently available for a couple hours in the evening. Leiv thought the bar usually had cars out front.

Besides the overall lack of hustle and bustle at TGS, and the fact Jack was a marvelous chef—Leiv was also quite fond of, and very comfortable seated within, the special "hideout booth"—as dubbed by Glover's mother Margaret Deers. *Several years back now.* This particular booth was the last seating available, way in the back, near the door to the restrooms and kitchen entrance. In this booth, you could "hide," physically and conversationally. Though tonight, there weren't any other patrons to "hide" from.

And here I am again, in the middle of "something"—back in TGS's hideout booth.

Brad asked, "Did this Tim Frasier at the hospital tell you anything new?"

Glover still didn't look up, but did shake his head and mumble, "Only that he didn't like Anthony Janus either. Said he was a bully."

Leiv and the two deputies quietly waited while Glover finished reading the report. When he eventually finished and looked up, Glover said in full voice, "Well, it's murder as far as I'm concerned. But not one bit of evidence in this report. And nothing from our interviews pointing toward anyone in particular."

"Like what kind of evidence?" Leiv was quick to ask, wanting to know what Glover was exactly looking for.

"Fingerprints, an empty vile of some prescription medicine with cardiac glycosides in it, someone with opportunity, motive, suspicious actions...."

Walker speculated, "Maybe they all planned and executed it together?"

Brad enhanced his fellow Deputy Sheriff's idea. "And the Route 66 tour was a planned way of pulling it off?"

Walker nodded.

Leiv couldn't pinpoint or articulate why, but his

current hunch was Marta and Gillian had been in cahoots. But he kept his mouth shut.

From Brad again, but with a theory different from Walker's, he said, "My money's on the guy in the hospital. And he hit his head on purpose."

"My money is on Tom 'Z Man' Carter," Glover finally said.

"Because?" Leiv pressed.

Glover laughed, bestowed a bemused and ironic smile Leiv's way, then answered, "Beats me. Just a hunch."

Leiv teased back, "But you're Shiné's Chief of Police. Hunches aren't allowed."

All four men laughed.

What else can we do?, Leiv thought. *One dead man, we aren't even sure it's murder, and with five suspects if it is...and no clues.*

"I fear," Glover said, summing up the implication of their collective suppositions, "this is going to be a tricky one, and I'm not sure if we'll ever figure it out."

"Well, before we eat, I have something to add to this conversation on another dead body," Leiv announced, thinking the time was now right.

Glover looked across the table at him with a skeptical expression.

Undeterred, Leiv looked back directly at Glover. "You might want to call your Captain friend in Adelanto. I know who killed his victim."

Now Glover turned his head sideways, with a questioning look on his face—though Leiv thought he still saw a touch of amusement in the chief's eyes.

"You remember the guy you and Walker were talking about just this morning in your office? The dead body you didn't like seeing?"

A nod from Glover.

Leiv explained about the couple at DAD's with the "boots," cowboy hat, and slightly different wife. "Had a case once in a lower court in Chicago. I was filling in for a friend. Open and shut case per the prosecution."

He looked around to include Brad, and Walker. *Yes,* he now had their full attention. "A middle-aged lady and a young adult man went into an upscale jewelry store. He was looking for an engagement ring, and his future mother-in-law was coming along to help him select a piece her daughter would like. After they finally picked a ring, the young man said he suddenly had to go to the bathroom. The owner looked up for a moment to point toward the back door that led to the restroom, then watched as the young man hurried off."

Glover gave him a "what the heck are you talking about" look, but waited without interrupting him.

"When the owner looked back down to the counter, the ring was gone."

"The kid stole it right there under his nose?" Walker asked.

Brad added with disbelief in his tone, "While he was looking up?"

Thinking back, Leiv now recalled the rather dramatic courtroom scene when the detective—whose face he could still visualize—presented his findings.

Leiv continued his background story. "Well, a diligent First District police detective on the case was an enterprising sort. With the facts I had, the case seemed open and shut to me at first. Well, when he testified in court, the detective had found out there were numerous cases over the last couple years in jewelry stores on the North Side where a matronly sort goes into a jewelry store to pick out a ring with a young man..."

"And the ring disappears in all the cases?" Walker leaned forward staring at Leiv, a slightly crooked and bemused smile on his lips. "They were in it together?"

"If I remember right, there were also several jewelry store insurance investigators testifying, too. The woman always wore fifties-style heavy white gloves, and the upshot was she would palm the ring into her glove. Everyone was always focused on the young man, not on her."

"The men?"

"Hired off the street. I think I heard a few years later, they finally tracked down one of them who confirmed the information presented that day in court."

Glover leaned forward and pressed Leiv, "And this applies to my Sheriff friend assigned to Adelanto?"

"Everyone's focused on the woman being different. She looks different somehow. But the man, well there was no doubt about him because of the boots and hat."

A big smile started spreading across Glover's face. "It was a different man. A 'replacement' for her now dead husband. All she had to do was change her hair, or makeup, or clothes. And all he had to do was put on the boots and hat."

Leiv finished, "And who here in Shiné at DAD's would think to connect them to an unknown victim in Adelanto? Everyone was left to follow and trust their deceiving eyes and conclude it was a different woman."

Walker looked pleasantly surprised, Brad seemed excited, and Glover covered his mouth with his hand to mask a probable smile. Above his hand his eyes twinkled.

After a couple minutes—during which they continued to think about what Leiv had postulated—Chef Jack and his wife Becca appeared from through the kitchen door carrying two covered platters.

Chapter Six

Brothers

From LC's journal: *I just can't imagine marrying no other woman than my Viola.*

Early Saturday Morning Shiné Police Station office:

Leiv's Saturday morning at Shiné Police Station started with just the two of them.

Glover leaning back in his comfy swivel chair staring at the ceiling, and Leiv, his back to Glover, standing wide-legged in front of the office's front window looking out onto Main Street.

This time, Leiv's attention—similar to Glover's Friday morning, was focused on Nate's bookstore directly across the street in front of him. He'd stood at Glover's window many a time previously, but usually staring at Le Bric-à-Brac, a couple store-fronts south of Nate's. Not that Nate's store-front building wasn't impressive—with its period-evoking red-brick face, and 1930s-style glass entry door—sided by two large glass display windows. But Le Bric-à-Brac, with its beautifully curved front window, was the star of main street. And his thoughts usually were not only on Mary Jones, but also encompassed all the enticing treasures he'd found within her store.

Leiv could still remember almost two years ago, standing beside Mary, admiring that crater-pocked blue "Hobnail Penny Perfume Bottle" as she held it up in the morning light streaming through that very window. *And here I am, again taking in Le Bric-à-Brac and Mary Jones's impact on my Shiné life...another spring, involved with Glover and Shiné shenanigans.* Leiv smiled with his thoughts. Clearly, he was moving past his crossroads dilemma.

"We still don't have anything," Glover said to the ceiling.

Leiv didn't turn from the window. "But we think one of them killed him."

"Yep."

"But like we said earlier...there's no real evidence he *was* poisoned. We really can't prove for sure he *was* murdered. All we know is he probably didn't need that drug."

Leiv looked for a moment at the maturing sunrise above Main Street, admiring the Mojave Desert morning colors. Then noticing Nate open his front door from the inside, he brought his attention back directly in front of him.

He watched Nate bring out—one at a time and seemingly struggling—two olden-styled fold-up wooden tables and set them up in front of his windows. Indeed, the tables looked very heavy, and antique in character. *Perfect for books,* Leiv thought admiringly.

Leiv felt more than heard Glover come over and stand for a moment behind him, then move to beside him. Also looking out across Main, watching Nate set up.

"Getting started early today," Leiv said, remembering Glover's desire to leave early yesterday like Nate. In unison, and clearly likeminded, Leiv and Glover both turned their heads to look first north, then south down Main. Not a car nor human being in sight. Unnecessarily, and *sotto voce*, Leiv murmured, "As if it makes any difference when he opens."

Glover chuckled, then said, "I did tell you, right? CHP picked up 'cowboy hat and boots' this morning."

Clearly pleased, the two men—brothers in mind and thought—stood quietly for several long moments.

Shiné. The clarity Leiv had been searching for in his LC's cupola hit home again. And *again*, the answer was easy. *Shiné is now my home.*

Before Leiv could dwell on his renewed resolve and plan further—in consort, one right behind the other—two sheriff jurisdiction patrol cars pulled up in front of Glover's office.

Deputies Brad Temper and Walker Johns each got out of their separate cars, and entered the office together. They could barely contain themselves.

Walker rushed to speak first. "We're damned sure Donny Latimer did it."

Leiv made a questioning face, and Glover didn't move.

"We think he was bullied, and my nephew's teacher said being bullied leaves scars kids never recover from."

"Yeah," Brad agreed nodding vigorously, making him look younger than Leiv knew the seasoned deputy was.

71

"But at least he ended up having a wife, who looked to me like she loves him and probably helped him with those emotional scars...."

Everything leaves scars, Leiv thought. He remembered the many wives he'd seen in court, who excused their husbands of many misdeeds because of perceived childhood scars of some type. Some included murder.

In the present, Brad added, "And that bullying would never be forgotten experiences." Then after a slight pause added, "I'd bet you my next paycheck, Donny knew who that group was from the start of the tour." He was looking directly at Glover.

"I doubt if we'll ever know..." Leiv pointed out the obvious. "But for what it's worth, I agree with you on the picture you've laid out. But what's all this about Donny Latimer being an abused kid? Where did you get that from?"

"Chicago of course." His chest visibly rose. "Our Sheriff is darned good, has a lot of friends, and talked to several pals back in Illinois."

Brad and Walker both walked over to the desk facing Glover's, and put their Smokey-the-Bear hats on the desk. Walker sat, while Brad continued to stand and explain what his "idol" boss dug up. "Had to go all the way back to microfiche, but he did find out the tour guide's mother lodged a harassment charge against some kids Donny— Dominic—went to school with. Even found a complaint she lodged against the school."

Wondering where that kind of record would be, Leiv inclined his head quizzically.

"Lots of old documents and records were compiled by the Archdiocese regarding priests and child molestation charges. Nothing like that with this kid, but the school did have to give them a dump of parent complaints. All kinds."

Glover finally commented, "Your Sheriff must really have good contacts?" His tone conveyed he was impressed.

"Actually, Chief, it's his pal in Chicago who has all the connections."

Leiv kept his mouth shut on the topic of Illinois politics and connections. *Heck, connections are why Adeleine is here staying with me....*

"So," Brad continued, "all five of the tour group on this trip are from Chicago."

"And don't tell me," Glover said, "they all went to the same school."

Brad shook his head. "Can't say, no records found on them yet except birth and social security and property stuff. But they're all the same age."

Leiv re-pictured the group from yesterday in his mind's eye. Admittedly he hadn't seen the table group for that long, or that close. Still, he said, "Didn't all look the same age to me. Luck of the draw I guess, when it comes to the wrinkle and saggy skin stuff." He sighed and wondered if Adeleine saw him as an old man. Unconsciously, he rubbed the skin under his chin and down his neck as if he was feeling for wrinkles, or the lack thereof. Leiv's fingers did encounter some disconcerting pouches. His law enforcement officer friends ignored his wrinkles comments and continued discussing information connections.

Leiv looked back out onto Main Street for a bit, watching as Nate carted out books from inside his store to fill his table tops—making several trips with an overloaded kid's red wagon.

M.M. Gornell

Turning back and rejoining the conversation, Leiv asked, "Are you all coming tonight? It is Saturday night you know. Shindig time…right, Walker?"

Chapter Seven

Familiar Territory, AKA The Gathering, AKA Shindig

From LC's journal: Sometimes it's really hard a figuring out what's important and what ain't. Viola is good at it. Me, only middlin.

Saturday Night: LC's Withdrawing Room

Oddly, Leiv hadn't noticed before—but did tonight. Above LC's monstrous fireplace, flickering light—from what was probably the last real wood fire of the season— seemed to be dancing on LC's withdrawing room ceiling. And that animated yellowish glow added another element of pleasure to his savoring this evening.

For on this Saturday night, Leiv was experiencing LC's withdrawing room with all his senses on high alert. *Yes*, tonight the ambiance LC and Viola created was working its magic, big-time. He almost spoke aloud to complement them across the great divide, but caught himself in time.

He was not only appreciating the total visual impact of Viola and LC's vision of a genteel drawing room—but also experiencing their world on a unique sensual level. Leiv felt he was *taking-in* the feel of textures, *taking-in* the smooth wood finishes, *taking-in* the nap of the woven tapestry, and *taking-in* the smooth leather seating upholstery.

And all—encapsulated in a current-time layer of enticing aromas generated by Hester and Adeleine's lovingly prepared hors d'oeuvre covering the low and over-sized antique oak coffee table that centered Leiv's Saturday night "shindig" in Rhodes Castle's "Withdrawing Room." *LC's pride and joy.*

"Thank you for bringing these glasses out again," Pastor Lloyd Apply said while placing his just-drained aperitif glass down next to the bottle of Harvey's Bristol Crème on LC's nested Edwardian tables. Then after a contented sigh, the pastor changed the topic. "Seems like we can't keep you out of trouble." He chuckled lightly. "Almost from the day you got here."

He and Apply were sitting in their customary well-worn armchairs, in their customary spots flanking LC's beautifully stacked and cherished Edwardian side-tables. Remembering back, Leiv forced himself not to look at HM sitting on the loveseat to his right. *My nemesis from those early days.* He did turn to his left a bit toward his friend, smiled, and said in a low voice, "I blame it all on Glover."

Leiv also sighed contentedly, founded in a momentary wave of pleasure. All was as it should be for

Leiv's Saturday night "gathering" in LC's cherished withdrawing room.

If you don't count an unsolved murder hanging in the air.

"I know you like those glasses." Leiv shifted his weight so he could turn even more directly toward Apply. "I think I mentioned before, Adeleine found the box holding those glasses in the kitchen on a lower back shelf?"

"Hand-blown you found out," Shiné's pastor reminisced with Leiv.

Margaret Deers and Adeleine were sitting in their now customary spots on the loveseat perpendicular to Apply's armchair—within earshot of Leiv and Apply's comments.

"Yes," Margaret contributed, after an appreciative sip from her own delicately stemmed glass. "I agree, and have remarked before myself—beautiful glasses, and good stuff." She leaned forward and out slightly in front of Adeleine, so she could more easily talk to Leiv directly where he sat at the head of their U-shaped gathering. "You know, Leiv, from what you, Walker, and my son have told us, it has to be the Tim guy. He was sitting the closest to Tony Janus."

Not necessarily in agreement with her conclusion, Leiv nodded in understanding of her reasoning. And still enjoying his "savory" moments, he looked around for a couple more seconds—taking it all in. In the past, attendees had varied—and sometimes extra chairs were brought in.

But few or many, Leiv thought, *it's a tradition I've started here. Our U-shaped setup and its feel of camaraderie, and the multi-topic discussions we've had.*

He had come to love how they were centered on LC's grand stone fireplace and hearth, with its perfectly accompanying Anatolia Terrain hearth-rug in front. Dobie was now coming regularly with Hester and David to queenly take her place on that very rug—clearly content to live with Hester, but also happy to "visit" her rug regularly.

Looking at Dobie laying in front of the fireplace—he thought fondly, that the icing on the cake for him in the Hester saga and Mojave Stone quest, was the added pleasure of knowing one of LC's Mojave stones was hidden just above Dobie, in plain sight, right in the center of the broad rock surface of the fireplace. Leiv forced back a smile—and fancifully interpreted Dobie's expression as smiling, too. *Her reasons unknown.*

"So the murderer is going free...," Adeleine, sitting next Margaret, said in a questioning tone.

Glover, sitting squeezed in to Leiv's right, said, "Not necessarily," though he shook his head, and sighed loudly. "Talked to the Sheriff before driving out here. No new evidence. Every one of those folks on that tour have what Hollywood-land calls 'squeaky-clean' pasts." He shook his head again. "Nothing." Then he leaned forward a bit so he could catch Brad's eye where he sat with Walker on a recently-added small divan next to Hester and Adeleine's loveseat. "But Brad's got a line of inquiry still going out in Chicago-land."

Deputy Sheriff Brad Temper smiled and nodded. "And I'll keep digging, looking into their pasts, questioning."

"Yep, even when that group gets back to the Midwest, they'll be peppering them with questions. If there is something there, maybe, eventually, one of them will let something slip." Glover's tone was wishful. He dropped back in his padded rocker.

The rocker the Chief of Police was now sitting in was an addition to LC's withdrawing room consequent of the movie-making crew sendoff. An armless parlor chair was a last-minute accommodation for the number of people that night—and makeshift for sure. At the time, it was a place to fit Glover into the group. That night, the Chief had taken to the spot next to Leiv, but not taken to the chair.

Consequently, the following day, Glover searched the castle—top to bottom including all the bedrooms on both sides of the grand staircase, and eventually came up with a small antique-looking rocker. Leiv initially thought it too small for Glover's substantial frame. And it did turn out to be a snug fit, but the little-looking rocker seemed to contour perfectly to his half-brother's body. And since that first Saturday after the movie maker's goodbye party, "the little rocker" as Leiv called it—even with its rather faded upholstery, had worked great.

"Want a refill, Lloyd?" Leiv asked.

To his left, the pastor shook his head.

"Think I will," Leiv said, accepting his own offer.

"I'm going to be a writer," Douglas "Hermit" Chan said loudly from his squeezed-in position next to Mary Jones and Doctor Will Walker on the loveseat down from Glover—facing Margaret and Adeleine on the other side of the center tables and munchies.

Leiv didn't have a clue what Hermit was talking about, but he leaned forward in his armchair and smiled encouragingly at him.

"You see," Hermit said looking meaningfully around the room, "after noticing those boots and that hat and the travel-group death, I'm thinking I could start writing mysteries—sort of in line with crazy real incidents like that."

Margaret scoffed kindly. "Who would believe something like that—"

"Well, it's happening, isn't it?" Hermit retorted, equally kindly.

Margaret nodded and admitted, "You have a point, Hermit—but do you have any writing experience?"

Hermit shook his head. "Who needs it…?"

"And what about that proposal you had me lugging around for the county for some kind of camera obscura thing?"

"I still plan to do that, too. No matter what the county says."

Leiv smiled and said, "From what I've seen of you, Hermit, you can do whatever you want." He raised his just-recently-filled aperitif glass in the air to his friend. "Much success."

"Do you have a penname?" Adeleine asked.

"Ockham." After smiling at her, Hermit looked back directly at Leiv and winked. "Always liked the sound of William of Ockham's name."

Huh? Was Hermit really talking about the man, or the subsequent paradigm, Occam's Razor? Leiv smiled to himself at yet another strange connection. Indeed, how could Hermit know he'd just been thinking about Occam's Razor yesterday? *Omen of something? Or was the man also psychic?*

"And what about your camera obscura?" Leiv forced back a memory of him and his deceased wife, Melissa, in Buckingshire on a tour viewing such a device. Leiv said, "I have seen one a long time ago. Marvelous."

Mary Jones, sitting between Hermit and Will, was now openly holding Doctor Will Walker's hand. "I'm thinking Shiné might be an energy hot-spot story."

"There are the ley lines...," Margaret mused.

"Then D&D's Tours and their ilk can go tromp around there in the future, instead of wanting to come here." Leiv knew his tone betrayed his ire, and dared not look at Glover next to him for fear he might be smirking — and making him even more miffed.

"Mother, you believe in that ley lines stuff?" Glover asked, his tone incredulous.

Leiv retained his smile knowing an interesting discussion was about to begin. And he was definitely looking forward to talking more, and continuing to "savor."

Still, he had to fight back the niggling feeling they were all missing something on the D&D Tours death front.

Epilogue

In Donny Latimer's experience, the types of requested Route 66 destination tours were faddish. A word of mouth thing for a year or so—then "the word" would change. Amboy and the crater one year, Kelso Station and the dunes the next. Side trips to Las Vegas, or to the Hoover Dam were big a couple years back. Even the Grand Canyon auxiliary loops were a "big thing" for awhile—but these days, Donny seldom got a request for his "loop tour"— straight out to Vegas, then back south and on to the featured Grand Canyon—the "grand-finale" as he liked to call it. Then heading back to Santa Monica on the south leg of his loop on I-40 and stretches of the old Route 66, stopping at places like Ludlow and Newberry Springs.

Consequently, after a long traveling-hiatus—they were now shepherding a van full of New Yorkers wanting a full loop tour. Donny was quite pleased to be mid-tour and once again standing on the rim of the Grand Canyon looking out into its vast greatness with his dear wife.

A few moments to ourselves, for me and Delyth.

This trip was an out-of-the-blue online request to take a band of fifteen travelers on a sorority sisters' reunion trip. The ladies were from NYC, so as was the norm, they'd flown to the West Coast where Donny's tour started at Santa Monica Pier. From there, he headed out along I-15 with a mix of freeway driving and actual "old road" driving in sections when he could.

Now, three days later, and actually at the Grand Canyon, their tour group of travelers had been handed over to a Park Ranger, allowing Donny and Delyth to be alone as they stood next to each other at the rim lookout—holding hands reminiscent of their early days of youthful love, while looking out into the canyon's magnificence together.

Most of the hard work part of their tour was behind them. On top of that, this was what Donny thought of as a "Deluxe" tour, and had charged accordingly. Hence the tour guide with them now. Also in line with the tour cost and his high standards for service, all rooms, rest stops, and restaurants were prearranged. These New York ladies had not complained about the price, had exalted the service Donny and Delyth were providing, and had openly stated they were getting a bargain and were enjoying themselves immensely.

They'd been to Vegas already, stopping at several casinos, staying the nights at The Orleans—then headed out to Hoover Dam. The Canyon was the last leg. *Another darned good tour attraction all by itself,* Donny thought.

On the way back—returning on I-40, they would be stopping at Don Laughlin's casino. But farther along on his loop back to Santa Monica Pier, Donny was definitely *not* planning on stopping at DAD's. *I've had enough of that place!*

All in all, he considered The Loop Tour a nice trip, with a mix of old scenic roads and fast moving freeway driving—and on a route he'd laid out in the startup exciting days of establishing D&D Tours. Gave him a nice feeling.

Indeed, for him, little had changed on his loop tour—except for heavier traffic. And, the sad fact the Summit Inn had burned down in Cajon Pass—*loved that place.* Had been a favorite tour stop. *Not anymore.*

He sighed—laced with sad nostalgia, and current happiness.

Then thinking further as he looked out into the Grand Canyon, Donny said, "It really does live up to the hype." He inched closer to Delyth at his side, and squeezed her hand. "The Grand Canyon really is 'grand.'"

He felt a warm breeze brush his cheek, and wondered how this out-in-the-open canyon viewing spot might feel in the dead of winter. *No gentle breeze then. Or in the middle of the summer, for that matter.*

Delyth turned her entire body toward Donny and gave his hand a reciprocating squeeze. "After all these years, I still enjoy holding your hand."

During that moment, Donny felt like the luckiest man in the world. *The warmth from Delyth's hand...*then for a couple more moments of silent awe and appreciation—instigated by their canyon view and swell of love for each other—Donny and Delyth watched their wide-eyed sorority-sister tour group head out on their park-sponsored hike down a trail along the rim.

Donny sighed gently. He and Delyth would continue to have some more moments to themselves. "I love you," he wanted to say, but thought it too schmaltzy, given their oddly private-but-oh-so-public environment.

"You know, they *all* deserved to die," Delyth said, emphasizing the word *all*. "But Tony was the worst. Wish I'd had more time. I would have taken them all out. But putting what was left of my heart pills in his soda, then tossing my empty container out the window around Newberry Springs was all I could think of on the spot—once I realized the opportunity I had. Hoping I wouldn't get caught. Wish I'd known who they were before we started...but once I saw them...I realized who they were."

Donny wasn't immediately sure what he was hearing his wife say—and doubted she could actually be telling him something about Anthony's murder? Unconsciously he shook his head, as if to improve his ear-to-brain connection.

"It was so easy. Taking my prescription pills out of my purse and slipping them in his drink as I opened it for him. I could tell there were plenty in the palm of my hand to do the trick." She squeezed Donny's hand again.

"What...what?" he muttered. He turned so he could look his dear Delyth directly in the eyes. "You?" His tone was incredulous.

She laughed offhandedly. "Donny, Donny, Dearest Donny. You must remember telling me everything about those little horrors." Then she smiled, and looked lovingly at him. "Did you hear them call him Tony?"

He shook his head.

"Anthony...Tony."

Tony. Indeed, he had shared many of his awful grammar school moments with his beloved, told her their names. Described their looks even. *And she had been there for me—and listened.* With her help, his childhood trials had subsided to never forgotten bad memories. Instead of debilitating emotional traumas.

"Who else could it be besides me?" she asked. "Who else had control of the drinks except us? You know it wasn't you, so it had to be me. The answer was the most obvious, the straightest connection. Not complicated at all."

"But, but," he stuttered and thought of all the tests, questions, and the investigation done by the Shiné Police Chief—Donny couldn't bring up his name right off but remembered it began with a "G"—and his buddy, that castle-guy. "But they didn't hold us," he stammered.

"No evidence." Delyth chuckled ever so slightly, her amusement laced with gentle feminine sweetness. She repeated, "Donny, Donny," and she smiled lovingly again. "Dearest, I've never forgotten."

Dominic's thoughts raced, clicking off the faces of their tour members. Those couldn't be the same kids he'd cowered from in the bathroom? Could they? He tried remembering their names from way back then. At first, all he could remember was Tony. The he remembered, *of course, there was a Tom…and a Tim, maybe. So long ago.* Almost forgotten by him. *But never forgotten by Delyth.*

As surprised as Donny was, and initially horrified by the thought of what she had done, a crucial part of his heart was overwhelmed by the thought and emotion that his wife loved him so much. Glad even.

Delyth had spited his enemy. *Much better than Sister Luke or Sister Aquinas ever did. Delyth, my love, my avenger, my own warrior princess.*

Donny knew even then, in that unbelievable moment on the rim of the Grand Canyon, he would adjust to Delyth's revelation. Even love her more. *If that's possible.* Sometimes the right answer is the easiest answer. And the path to that easy answer is straight and direct. *Might be some kind of axiom to remember there?*

Still hand in hand—Dominic and Delyth decided on taking an unguided canyon viewpoint walk of their own— and as they slowly strode on the rim trail, they sang softly to each other…

He hath loosed the fateful lightning of His terrible swift sword;
His truth is marching on.
Glory! Glory! Hallelujah! Glory! Glory! Hallelujah!
His truth is marching on.

Never Forgotten
In Their Order of Appearance or Mention

Characters with Novel of Their First Appearance

Dominic	Rhodes—Never Forgotten
Donny Latimer	Rhodes—Never Forgotten
Delyth Latimer	Rhodes—Never Forgotten
Martalina "Marta" Minor	Rhodes—Never Forgotten
Anthony "Mr. T" Janus	Rhodes—Never Forgotten
Oliver" Ollie" —Llewellyn	Rhodes—Never Forgotten
Adler "Mack" Wayne	Rhodes—Never Forgotten
LydiaRose "The Manchester Woman"	Rhodes—Never Forgotten
Josephine "Josie"	Rhodes—Never Forgotten
Della-Louise	Rhodes—Never Forgotten
Leigh-Everett "Leiv" Rhodes	Rhodes—The Mojave-Stone
Margaret Deers	Rhodes—The Mojave-Stone
Adeleine Moore	Rhodes—The Caretakers
Lucien "Lucca" Fabero	Rhodes—The Caretakers
Chief of Police Glover "Dusty" Deers	Rhodes—The Mojave-Stone
Deputy Walker Johns	Rhodes—The Mojave-Stone
Hester Miller-Milhouse - "HM"	Rhodes—The Mojave-Stone
Douglas "Hermit" Chan	Rhodes—The Movie-Maker
Mary Jones	Rhodes—The Mojave-Stone
Gillian "Gill" Butté	Rhodes—Never Forgotten
Tom "Z-Man"Carter	Rhodes—Never Forgotten
Tim "Backup" Frasier	Rhodes—Never Forgotten
Deputy Sheriff Brad Temper	Rhodes—The Mojave-Stone
Chef Jack	Rhodes—The Mojave-Stone
Becca	Rhodes—The Caretakers
Pastor Lloyd Apply	Rhodes—The Mojave-Stone
Dr. William "Will" Walker.	Rhodes—The Mojave-Stone
David Milhouse	Rhodes—The Movie-Maker
Dobie	Rhodes—The Mojave-Stone

ACKNOWLEDGEMENTS

As always, my gratitude goes to my excellent editor—Kitty Kladstrup. This story would not be published without her.

To my relatives, friends, fellow authors, and readers—thanks for your continuing words of encouragement. I can never properly say how much your support means to me.

I'm also most grateful to my Route 66 and Public Safety Writers Association (PSWA) friends and business owners who always so graciously provide information on animals, politics, law-enforcement, Route 66, and local lore. I continue to be connected to many electronically.

And to my dear editor for so long, Virginia Moody,
whose "angel spirit" still continues with me in my
heart—thank you for being my friend.
You will never be forgotten.

Madeline (M.M.) Gornell's mystery novels include—PSWA award winners *Uncle Si's Secret* and *Lies of Convenience* (also a Hollywood Book Festival Honorable Mention), *Death of a Perfect Man*, and *Reticence of Ravens* (a finalist for the Eric Hoffer 2011 fiction Prize, the da Vinci Eye for cover art, and the Montaigne Medal for most thought-provoking book). *Counsel of Ravens* (a London Book Festival Honorary Mention and LA Book Festival Runner-Up) is her first sequel, and was a continuation of Hubert Champion's Mojave saga.

Rhodes—Never Forgotten is the fourth novel in her second series featuring Leiv Rhodes's Mojave saga that began in *Rhodes—The Mojave-Stone.*

She continues to be inspired by travelers on historic Route 66, and these, her continuing Rhodes novels, reflect that fascination. Madeline lives with her husband and assorted canines in the Mojave High Desert near the internationally revered Route 66.

e

From LC's journal, on page one-hundred-and-two, where Leigh Cooper Rhodes explains the origin of his town's name—Shiné.

Viola likes to show our boys the stones in morning light. Sitting as they do up top of the house, mornings usually, letting the sun make them glitter, sparkle, shine. André calls it shiny, and it comes out his little mouth as shy-knee. Viola's got a soft spot for that one, and has started saying the name of our place shy-knee like the boy. She may have made shy-knee a reality, but it's little André who really named the place.

Thinking I'm gonna be changing the spelling too, and with one of them little marks at the end. Make it fancy, befitting a Leigh Cooper Rhodes kind of town.

Then he'd printed, in block letter across a whole page:

SHINÉ